The Sleeping Fire

by

DAPHNE CLAIR

TORONTO • LONDON • NEW YORK • AMSTERDAM
SYDNEY • HAMBURG • PARIS

Original hardcover edition published in 1979
by Mills & Boon Limited

ISBN 0-373-02292-1

Harlequin edition published October 1979

"Obviously I just don't turn you on,"

Adam said smoothly, as he let her go.

"No," Lee lied coolly, the feel of his firm sensual mouth still on hers. "Is this one of the things I have to put up with to keep my job?"

The sparks of anger in his eyes were quickly hidden. "Not at all," he said. "You wouldn't believe, I suppose, that I simply gave in to a natural impulse on finding a very attractive young woman in my arms."

She didn't believe for a moment that he was a man to give in to impulse. "I'll take care that you don't 'find me in your arms' again," she said tartly. "Thank you for the lunch."

He laughed softly. "I think I'm going to enjoy having you work for me...."

CHAPTER ONE

LEE PALMER paused in adjusting the curtain behind her desk to screen the January sun, and for a few moments admired the view. The building where she worked was a quite modern multi-storey one, and past the shops and offices of Auckland's heart the Waitemata harbour sparkled in the morning sunlight, with Rangitoto rising gracefully from its waters in the distance. Hard to believe that the island volcano had once risen, spitting clouds of flame and hurling molten rocks as far as the mainland, from the ocean floor; and that only seven or eight hundred years ago, well within the racial memory of the Maori people, it had still been active, its angry flame burnishing the waters of the harbour.

Helen Carter, the secretary Lee shared with Patricia Blyth, *Lively Lady*'s editor, poked her curly head around the door, and Lee turned.

'He's *here*!' Helen hissed dramatically. 'The New Broome! He's just gone into Pat's office.'

Hiding slight alarm, Lee said, 'Well, he can't eat us, can he?'

'Can't he, though?' Helen asked cryptically. Glancing behind her as though to forestall being pounced on, she said, 'They say he's a terror.' Muttering that she had better look busy, she shut the door.

Wryly, Lee reflected that 'They' had been saying so ever since the news broke that Carson & Company, publishers of several magazines, had been taken over by Broome Associates. Rumour said the firm had American connections. The new managing editor, a son of the original Broome, was supposed to have spent several years in the States and picked up some high-powered business methods there.

There did seem to be some basis for Helen's apprehension about the new boss, Lee supposed. No one at *Lively Lady* had as yet met the man, and Lee strove to keep an open mind. But such was the reputation that had preceded him that it became increasingly difficult not to have preconceived ideas. Adam Broome left his mark, and those on whom he left it so often described him in adjectives ranging from 'dynamic' to 'ruthless'—that the entire staff was in a state of nervous tension waiting for his first descent upon them. After news had filtered through from some of the other magazines' staffs of probing questions, drastic re-shuffles of staff and one or two early retirements, it was inevitable that some not-very-original wit would coin the nickname of 'New Broome' for Adam Broome. *Living at Home* and *Holiday News* had been thoroughly shaken up, by all accounts, and *Green Fingers*, the grapevine said, was likely to 'get the chop'. Now, apparently, it was *Lively Lady*'s turn for a visitation.

Lee, although noted for her calm efficiency, was not entirely immune to the air of apprehension that hung over the offices, and although she tried to be open-minded about the changes that had taken place in the firm, she had a distinct feeling that life was going to be less pleasant with Adam Broome in charge.

Determined not to allow the knowledge of his presence in the room next door to change her normal routine, she took up the small copper watering-can which stood on the filing cabinet in the corner of her office and carefully watered the kumara plant which trailed its heart-shaped leaves along the wall from its pottery container. To her annoyance, she jumped almost guiltily when the intercom on her desk buzzed as she was engaged in this task, and a small trickle of water landed on the carpet.

'Yes?' she said rather more crisply than usual, as she placed the can on her desk.

'Mr Broome is with me, Lee,' said the Editor's voice. 'Could you come in and help me to—to explain how we work?'

Help you to deal with the ogre, you mean, Lee thought humorously, detecting a slight note of apppeal behind the words. Pat Blyth had steered *Lively Lady* from undeniably shaky beginnings to the position of the most successful of Carson & Company's publications, holding second place among the national magazines aimed primarily at women. Lee was convinced she had nothing to fear from the New Broome, but as Pat's assistant editor for the last year, she had learned with surprise that the older woman was unexpectedly lacking in self-confidence, although she usually hid it well.

Quickly she checked her appearance in the full-length mirror built into the inside of the narrow closet in one wall. Dark brown hair was neat and glossy, cut in a page-boy shape that framed an oval face, lightly made up to gloss a faint summer tan. Eye make-up discreetly highlighted deep hazel eyes flecked with gold and brown in close-up, and accentuated naturally dark lashes and nicely shaped brows. Her lipstick looked fresh and clearly outlined a mouth that was attractive enough. Her grey shirt-style blouse and simple darker grey skirt looked neat and businesslike, like her medium-heeled light tan shoes.

Satisfied that she looked like an efficient assistant editor, she tapped on the door to Patricia Blyth's office and went in.

Her first thought was that he had been bullying Patricia, for the editor's eyes were anxious, and her cheeks faintly flushed. Her next thought, as she turned a rather hostile gaze on him, was that he didn't look like an ogre. His face was calm and quite good-looking, though not memorably so.

Then, as Pat introduced them and he stood to shake her hand, she saw that he was taller than she had thought, probably above six feet. It wasn't apparent until one stood close to him, perhaps because he had a relaxed, though not stooped, stance. Broad shoulders set off a well-proportioned masculine frame. A good tan enhanced his undoubted attraction.

His hand was firm and warm, and as she looked up to give a him a cool smile of greeting, she had an inkling of what 'they' meant when they spoke in slightly awed tones about this man. There was nothing startling about his features, although she noticed fleetingly that his mouth looked well-defined and firm, but his eyes met hers with an impact that startled her. They were blue and very probing, and when she stepped back as he released her hand, they made an impersonal but very thorough assessment of her from head to toe and back again. His mouth moved a little at the corner as his eyes returned to her slightly defiant stare, and he gave a little nod of seeming approval, which instantly antagonised her, and told her mildly to sit down.

The antagonism grew over the next hour. He was nothing if not thorough. He took them over every aspect of the magazine's production—policies, methods, deadlines, layouts, artwork, readership, advertising. There seemed to be nothing he did not want to know, although the financial aspect was apparently already at his fingertips, judging from some of the questions he asked.

He made very little comment, and if anything his face gave away less of what he was thinking as the morning progressed than it had at the beginning. But Lee was not stupid, and the trend of the questions showed the way his mind was working.

How much had the circulation increased in the past year or two? His dark-blond head nodded impassively as he digested the answer, and Lee had an intuitive feeling he had known. Only one women's magazine outsold *Lady*, after all ... Defending her chief, Lee reminded him of that.

Yes, he said smoothly, and mentioned by how much. He certainly did his homework, Lee admitted silently.

How long had the same writer been producing the 'Hearth and Home' column every week? Was the reader feedback favourable? Were there signs that 'Homelover' —he pronounced the writer's pseudonym with a hint of distaste—was getting stale?

Did they have a policy of encouraging promising new writers and artists, or did the sameness of the illustrations and writing styles he had noted in the back-copies he had been reading indicate that they were using the same ones year after year?

And the final, deadly question. How long had Miss Blyth been editing *Lively Lady*?

Lee, who had braved a few razor-sharp glances from his cold blue eyes to divert his attention from Patricia's flushed and flustered face and reply to some of these questions for her, could not answer this. She longed to hear her chief say something cutting like, *Since you were in short pants, young man!* For he would be in his early or

middle thirties, and she was fifty-seven, as Lee happened
to know.

But in answer to his soft-voiced question—and Lee had
to acknowledge that there was nothing hectoring in his
manner, in fact his voice seemed to grow more gentle as his
queries became more lethal—Pat said unhappily, 'Thirty
years.'

'That's an impressive record,' Adam Broome said
quietly. And he smiled. The smile was quite startlingly
attractive, making deep creases beside his mouth and
showing very nice teeth. It even seemed to warm his eyes.
But although Patricia smiled back in a slightly bemused
way, Lee sat stiffly wary, her own mouth firmly closed. She
didn't trust this man, and she didn't like him, and she
was very sure that the smile was as the smile on the face
of a tiger.

Helen brought in cups of tea, and Lee noted the slight,
amused quirk at the corner of his mouth as the visitor—
except, she reminded herself, that he wasn't a visitor, he
was their new boss—was handed one of the dainty china
cups and invited to help himself to milk and sugar from
a matching jug and sugar-basin. She was sure he was
seeing them as a symbol of the out-of-date magazine they
were producing.

Forgetting the tentative attempts she had made herself to bring a more modern approach to parts of *Lively
Lady*, she was possessed of a lively indignation that led her
to stir her sugar into her tea with more vigour than was
warranted, so that it slopped into the saucer. She glanced
up to find Adam Broome watching her with apparent interest, and was further annoyed because he had noted her
small clumsiness. *He*, she noticed, didn't take sugar at all.
He wouldn't! she concluded with unnecessary venom.

Sweetening would be the last thing he wanted.

Later they showed him round and introduced him to everyone, and then Patricia remembered an appointment, explaining in what Lee considered to be quite unnecessary detail that it was a business appointment, and exactly why she couldn't cancel it.

Adam Broome was perfectly polite about it, almost soothing in fact, and Patricia went off, leaving him, with an apologetic glance, in Lee's office.

Not having the faintest clue what to do with him, Lee said briskly, 'Won't you sit down, please, Mr Broome?'

She saw him glance at the copper watering-can that still rested on her desk, and she moved it back to the filing cabinet as he looked around the rest of the room, his gaze coming back to her as she sat down behind the desk.

'Is there anything else you would like to know?' she asked.

'Yes,' he said, immediately. 'I would like to know what your ideas are on improving this magazine.'

'*Mine?*'

'That's right.' He seemed quite at ease in the chair opposite hers, his hands resting lightly on its upholstered arms. He had well-shaped hands with long fingers and nails clipped short, and although she supposed he did little manual work, they were very masculine and didn't look in the least soft.

Realising she was avoiding his eyes, she raised hers to his face and said, 'I don't see why you want *my* ideas.'

He said softly, 'I don't need a reason'—and she supposed that was a reminder that he was the man in charge now—'but if you want one, you're young and presumably you didn't get to be assistant editor by being dimwitted; you look reasonably with-it and from the little I've seen this morning I'd say that far from being dim, you're highly intelligent and efficient. So I'm very sure that you must have some ideas of your own.'

'When I do, I pass my suggestions on to Miss Blyth,' she said stiffly.

'Who doesn't take them.'

'I didn't say that,' she said coldly.

'You didn't have to. It's perfectly obvious that no really innovative changes have been made in the magazine for the last ten years or more.'

'If you have a successful formula,' she said, 'why change it? You do know that *Lady* is the firm's top seller?'

He said, with the first sign of impatience she had seen, 'Yes. Also the country's *second* best seller in the field. Second-best might be good enough for Carsons—Broomes like to be first.'

I'll bet they do, she thought. *And you're going to make sure that they are.* She took another look at his impassive face and revised her first opinion of it as unmemorable. He might not be wonderfully handsome, but his mouth and chin had a definite cast of power, and no one could ignore those compelling eyes. At the moment, surprisingly, they held a gleam of humour that was echoed in the small tug at the corner of his mouth.

'So——' he said, apparently reading the expression on her face. 'You don't like me, Miss Palmer. Too bad. But if you want to keep your job you'll just have to grin and bear it, won't you?'

'I don't think I've given you any reason to think that——' she began, shaken by his brutal frankness, but determined not to show it.

'My dear girl,' he said with something approaching

boredom, 'it sticks out a mile. Your lovely face, in case you didn't know, is very expressive.'

Her *lovely* face? Lee wondered if that was an unthinking cliché, because certainly nothing had led her to think that he admired her.

'Oh, yes, I *had* noticed,' he said softly, the gleam in his eyes intensifying. 'Beauty, intelligence, and loyalty for starters,' he mused, openly enjoying her astonishment now. 'I wonder what else lies under that nun-like outfit.' His eyes passed faint disparagement over her clothes.

'Scepticism!' she snapped, because in spite of herself he was disturbing her, and she strongly suspected his motives.

He glanced at the handsome wrist-watch he wore and suddenly stood up. 'Supposing I take you out to lunch and find out,' he said, coming to her side of the desk and pulling out her chair so that she had no choice but to stand too. She couldn't tell whether it was by accident or design, but when she rose the chair was behind her at an angle that made it impossible to pass by it. Adam Broome was standing between the desk and the wall on the other side, fingering a leaf of her kumara plant. She took a tentative step that brought her close to him, expecting him to move back out of her way, but he didn't. He turned his head instead and said, 'Is this the reason for the watering-can?'

'Yes,' she said, not moving back because that would have looked silly. He wasn't touching her and there was no reason for her breath to be catching in her chest, but it was, and she was very much aware of the masculinity of the hand that finally stopped fingering the leaf and dropped to her waist to guide her before him as they went round the desk.

'Is this a business lunch?' she asked bluntly, moving away from his light touch and turning to face him.

She received the full force of his smile, which was really unfairly devastating, considering she didn't even like the man.

'What else?' he said smoothly. 'Don't you have me down as a hard-headed businessman whose every move is calculated to increase my wealth and power?'

'Just so long as I know,' she said, taking her bag from the closet and hanging it over her shoulder.

He gave a low laugh as he opened the door for her.

They ate salad and seafood in a good restaurant close to the office, and he ordered wine which Lee drank sparingly. When she put her hand over her glass he said softly, 'Are you afraid I'm plying you with wine to pry confidences from you?'

She shook her head, smiling a little, because he was being good company and the food and wine must have mellowed her a little towards him. 'It makes me sleepy, and I have to work this afternoon.'

'Conscientious,' he murmured, with such patent approbation that she had to laugh.

He leaned back in his chair and watched her, his own glass in one hand. Perhaps it was the wine, but his eyes were far from cold now, and she felt warmth flood through her at the look in them. 'Of course, *I* could give you the afternoon off,' he said.

Coupled with the look in his eyes, she wasn't at all sure what that meant, and was immediately wary.

'And give you an excuse to sack me?' she said lightly. 'No, thanks, Mr Broome.'

'I wouldn't sack you,' he said. 'I brought you out for lunch because I want you to keep on working for the firm, and I hoped it would help you overcome your dislike of me.'

By overwhelming me with your fatal charm? she wondered. If so, she had to concede that he wasn't making too bad a job of it.

Aloud, she said, smiling, 'I can't be bribed with food and wine, Mr Broome.'

'Incorruptible, too,' he commented, his eyes faintly mocking. 'Or does the qualification mean you *can* be bribed with suitable inducements?'

'I don't really know,' she said. 'No one has ever tried.'

'Well, that's honest, anyway.' His look became slightly speculative. 'You tempt me to try,' he added.

'I didn't intend to,' she assured him, sure that to tempt this man in any way could be a dangerous game, although the tiger claws were well sheathed at the moment. She would prefer them to stay hidden.

Back at the office, Helen looked up with slight surprise as they entered together. She had already left for her own lunch before they went out.

Although he was right behind her, Lee didn't wait for Adam Broome to open the door of her own office, and as she went through the doorway rather quickly, she was halted with a jerk when the strap of her shoulder bag caught on the handle. Her companion cannoned into her, his hard body almost knocking the breath from hers. Then his arm was about her waist to steady her, and his other hand freed the bag and slid the strap from her shoulder as he took her with him into the room and shut the door. It all seemed to happen in the space of a second and she had no chance to move out of his hold before her bag thudded softly to the floor and his other arm encircled her and turned her fully to him.

Then his mouth was on hers, firm and warm and undeniably sensual. He held her very closely, and the thin shirt under her hands did little to mute the warmth of his body against hers. She found that she wanted desperately to respond to the insistent lips moving against her mouth, and to stop herself, she pushed against him with her hands.

Briefly his hold tightened, then he let her go, quite without haste.

He was smiling a little quizzically as she stepped back from his embrace, and there was an underlying satisfaction in his eyes that annoyed her intensely.

Automatically she picked up her bag and as he watched she dumped it on top of her desk and took out a tissue and wiped her mouth, trying to think of something cutting to say. She was twenty-four and couldn't claim never to have been kissed, but she was a great believer in kisses being part of a real relationship rather than a simple flaring of physical attraction between people who had only just met. Besides, she had a distinct feeling that this had been somewhat of an experiment on his part, though she was not at all sure what he had hoped to prove.

She replaced the tissue in her bag and said composedly, 'Do I take it this is another of the things I have to "put up with" if I want to keep my job?' Baiting the tiger was foolish, but her pride demanded it.

The spark of anger in his eyes was hidden so quickly she might have imagined it. But the quality of the smile he gave her was definitely nasty. 'Not at all,' he said smoothly. 'You could call it an attempt to find other inducements. But obviously I don't turn you on.'

'No,' she lied coolly.

'You wouldn't believe, I suppose, that I simply gave in to a natural impulse on finding a very attractive young woman in my arms.'

She didn't believe for a minute that he was a man who

gave in to impulse without a second thought, and she let him see her disbelief in her face. 'I shall take care that you don't "find me in your arms" again,' she said tartly. 'Thank you for the lunch.'

He laughed softly. 'I think I'm going to enjoy having you working for me.'

'I'm thinking of resigning,' she said.

'Rubbish! You love your job—that much I discovered over lunch.'

He had, too, she realised. He was, in fact, exasperatingly clever.

When he left to go in search of Miss Blyth she was profoundly relieved, but as the tension ebbed from her it left her feeling decidedly flat. It might not be easy working under the New Broome, but it promised to be remarkably stimulating, at least.

CHAPTER TWO

FOR a while it seemed that nothing drastic was going to happen, after all. The office continued as usual, except that Adam Broome was often there, watching without comment, making everyone work even harder than usual simply by the fact of being around. They became quite used to his presence, but Lee, for one, kept wondering when—and where—the axe was going to fall.

When it did, she wasn't really surprised.

Patrica called her into the other room to break the news.

'I'm not being *forced* to retire,' she insisted, in the face of Lee's indignation. 'But I just don't feel that I'm up to making the drastic changes that Mr Broome wants. He's been very nice about it, and financially extremely generous. I'll be able to have a real holiday, and then perhaps look for a rather less demanding job. Maybe something part-time.'

Lee could hardly argue, but she burned inwardly with anger. It might have been done with subtlety and with financial 'generosity', which she scornfully thought of as conscience money, but the fact remained that Pat had lost her job several years before retirement age; and in spite of her determined cheerfulness, new jobs at her age were extremely difficult to find.

Lee was so upset that it didn't even occur to her that she was next in line for the editor's job until Adam Broome came into her office that afternoon.

He didn't take the chair on the other side of her desk,

18

but leaned on the edge of the desk instead, saying, 'I believe Miss Blyth has told you she's retiring.'

'Yes,' she said shortly.

'You don't seem very pleased.'

'Should I be?' she flashed. Then, trying to control her temper, she added, 'She's a very good editor, and a friend. I like working with her.'

'She *was* a very good editor,' he corrected. 'Right now, she's past it.'

'Fifty-seven isn't exactly ancient, these days!'

'It is if one hasn't changed one's ideas in thirty years.'

'You might have given her a chance to try!'

'I did,' he said patiently. 'She didn't want to try. We had a perfectly amicable discussion and she's quite happy with the outcome, I assure you. So should you be. You're next in line, obviously.'

'For the chopping block?' she asked, deliberately misunderstanding him.

'For the job of editor.'

She was silent for a moment. Then she asked, 'Are you offering it to me?'

'Yes. It will mean an increase in salary for you, as well as much more responsibility—well, you know what the job entails.'

'How much of an increase?' she asked him, and felt her cheeks warm a little when he flashed her an amused glance. Did he think he had found the 'suitable inducement' with which she could be bribed—good old-fashioned money?

When he told her it was such a generous 'inducement' that she was slightly stunned and reacted with unnatural calm, not really taking it in.

'Well?' he asked.

'I don't know,' she said slowly. 'I'd like to think it over.'

'Two days,' he said. 'That's all I can give you.'

She had a date that night, with one of the journalists working on *Holiday News*. She had a lot in common with Brian Small and had been out with him several times before, but tonight she was abstracted, her mind busily turning over the problem of the offer of promotion, and over coffee in her small modern flat, he asked her what was bothering her.

'Oh, Brian, I'm sorry,' she said. 'I haven't been very good company tonight, have I?'

'You're always good company,' he said. 'But there's obviously something on your mind. Like to tell me?'

'I've been offered the job of editor of *Lady*.'

Brian looked impressed, then thoughtful. 'So—the Broome is going to sweep Pat Blyth under the carpet, is he?'

'She's resigned. Willingly, she *says*.'

'*Huh!*'

Lee smiled a little. 'Yes,' she said. 'That's what *I* thought.'

'Anyway, that's *her* problem, isn't it? Not yours. Aren't you going to jump at the chance?'

'I don't know. I just don't like getting it *this* way. Sort of over poor Pat's dead body. It makes me feel so—I suppose opportunist is the word.'

'Well, there's no denying it's an opportunity. But not of your own making. And I don't suppose Pat will object, will she? Not that she's in any position to do so, mind you ...'

'Oh, no, I'm sure she won't blame me.'

'And if you don't take the job, someone else will.'

'Yes, I think it's pretty clear that Pat is definitely out of the job, whatever I say.'

'Well then, where's the problem?'

No problem, really, she supposed, except that she wished she hadn't seen that gleam of laughter in Adam Broome's eyes when she had asked him to name the salary. The money was undoubtedly a temptation, and it was not only for herself that she wanted it. But she wished she did not have a sneaking feeling that Adam Broome would think he had bought her.

'I can do with the money,' she said ruefully.

'Who can't? It makes the world go round, these days.'

'I thought it was love that did that.'

'Not in the Broome's circles, honey. Although he's not short of either, by all accounts.'

'What do you mean by that?'

'Didn't you know? Not content with taking over old Carson's business, apparently he's taking over his daughter as well. You know—Lovely Lisbet, the gay divorcee. The Broome swept her right off her feet, I believe.'

'Oh, do stop talking in clichés!' Lee said rather snappily. Brian looked surprised and she said, 'Sorry! Please go on.'

'Well, that's about it, really. Lisbet and the Broome have been seeing quite a bit of each other, according to some who seem to know. Maybe he'll be her next husband.'

'She's only had one!' Lee protested mildly. 'You make it sound as though she changes them every week!'

'Well, the first one didn't last long, did he? About a year, wasn't it? And then he did a flit back to America, where he came from.'

Lee, who didn't really like discussing other people's affairs in this vein, shrugged. But she discovered that there was something she very much wanted to know, and Brian, with his journalist's instinct for gossip, might be the one to tell her. 'Will she be *his* second wife?' she asked casually.

'Uh-uh. Never married, dear. Maybe he thinks it's time he did.'

After Brian had gone, Lee wondered about that. Maybe if Adam Broome thought it was time he got married, he would set about it in the same cool, calculating way he conducted his business affairs. If he wanted someone suitable, he could hardly do better than Lisbet Carson. She *was* lovely to look at and at the few brief meetings Lee had had with her she seemed perfectly charming too. Her father was a widower and she had taken the place of a wife at company functions since she was only in her teens, so her social experience would no doubt be an asset to a man like Adam Broome. Her wedding had been quite a social occasion in itself, and Lee had been sad for her when the marriage broke up. And although Brian had called her a 'gay divorcee' Lee didn't think she had looked particularly gay since it happened. She was certainly seen about at parties and race meetings, and dressed as beautifully as always, but although her smile was as warm as ever, it seemed to lack its former sparkle. Maybe Adam Broome could bring that sparkle back.

Somehow, Lee doubted it, she told herself. He was very much a businessman, hard and clever and cold as granite. *Cold?* She was shaken by a sudden vivid memory of hard male warmth against her body, and firm lips moving sensually on hers.

Turning out the light over her bed as she climbed into it, she felt herself flushing in the darkness. It hadn't meant a thing to him, except a passing impulse. Ever since, he had been just as cool and distant as at their first meeting in Pat Blyth's office. And it certainly didn't mean a thing to her, except that she felt a strange prickling of her skin whenever he was near, a thoroughgoing awareness of his presence that she hoped sincerely she never betrayed. It was a purely physical reaction, she told herself, and she would get over it in time.

She didn't wait the two days that he had given her, but went to see him in his office on the next floor up the following morning. His secretary asked her to wait a few minutes, which gave her time to get ridiculously nervous, for no good reason that she could think of, and when she was allowed in she walked with her head held at a proud angle which made her look taller, because that was her usual reaction to nervousness, and her way of hiding it.

'I've decided I'll take the job,' she said, as soon as she sat down.

'Good,' he said after a moment. 'I'm glad you didn't keep me in suspense for the whole two days. Are you busy this evening?'

'Well—no,' she answered, thinking he wanted her to work overtime for some reason.

'I'll take you out to celebrate.'

His hard eyes held an expression she couldn't fathom. 'Is that an order—sir?' she said dryly.

'Yes. And you can call me Adam. That's an order, too,' he said, with a faint edge to his voice. 'Senior staff do.'

'Thank you,' she said quietly.

'Where do you live?'

She told him the address and he scribbled it on a pad on his desk.

'I'll pick you up,' he said. 'Do you like to dance?'

'Yes.'

'Fine. Will seven-thirty do?'

'Yes.' She quelled suddenly arising panic at the thought of dancing with him and tried to look ultra-calm. She might have succeeded in looking bored, for he cast her a glance that seemed faintly annoyed, but she told herself it wouldn't hurt him. No doubt plenty of women would have fallen about with gratitude if they received an invitation from him. Lisbet Carson, perhaps, for one. She wondered if Lisbet would object to his taking her out tonight. But it would easily be explained, of course. *'Business, darling. Keeping the staff happy,'* she could imagine him saying. The thought brought a sardonic little smile to her lips, and he said abruptly, 'What's funny?'

'Nothing. Just a—private thought.'

He looked as if he would have liked to make her disclose it, but apparently even he realised that thoughts were not the property of the boss.

'Come here a minute,' he said, and as she rose rather reluctantly and came around his desk, he pulled a couple of magazines from his drawer and placed them on the top. 'Look at these, and tell me if you think we can produce something like them.'

Lee would have preferred to take them back to her chair, but he was flipping over pages and pointing out features he wanted her to take note of, so she had to stand by his chair, her hand resting on the back of it, inches from his shoulder. With an effort she concentrated on the magazines.

They were American, and very well done, as she could see. Not of the very expensive variety which could be bought in bookshops in Auckland, but attractive in a more modest way. Some of the articles were controversial.

'Partly it would depend on the printer,' she was saying, when the telephone on his desk called his attention. She made to move away, but he grasped her wrist with his free hand to stop her, shaking his head slightly at her as he lifted the receiver and spoke into it. She made a small effort to pull away, but his grip remained firm and rather than make it into a small, undignified tug-of-war, she remained still and idly flipped over the pages she had already seen of the magazine in front of her, pretending not to notice that he was watching her, and determinedly ignoring the apparently absent-minded stroking of his thumb over the back of her hand.

A few minutes later he put down the phone and released her hand.

'Now,' he said crisply, 'what were you saying?'

It took her a moment or two to remember. 'It would depend partly on the printer,' she reiterated. 'They've made use of overprinting techniques and different shades of paper to make the copy look interesting.'

'What about the subject matter?' he asked. 'How do you think that would go down in New Zealand?'

'Some of it, quite well, I should think,' she said. 'I do think our readers might be ready to break away from the kitchen-and-kids type of article.'

'So you do think I'm right,' he said softly.

'I don't think we should change the publication too drastically or too suddenly,' she said. 'We have a lot of loyal readers who won't want to see it change at all. We could lose them, and not pick up enough new ones to replace them.'

'So you wouldn't approve of a big advertising campaign to launch a new-style *Lively Lady* in a radically different format?'

Considering that, she leaned back against his desk, her hands holding its edge on each side of her. 'Is that what you were thinking of?' she asked.

'It's one suggestion.'

'It sounds more like your style than a gradual change.'

'What would you know about my style?' he mocked gently.

'Well, you haven't exactly let the grass grow since you moved in here, have you?' she pointed out reasonably.

'Maybe I've been letting it grow more than you realise,' he said, and suddenly stood up, raising his hand to run a finger down her cheek and then lightly across her lips. His touch electrified her, but she didn't move because to straighten up from her lounging pose against his desk would bring her very close to him, and that was the last thing she wanted—with her mind, at least. She supposed she must look quite unconcerned.

'Come on,' he said, with a light touch on her arm. 'I'll take you down to Miss Blyth and break the news officially. Then she can start handing over to you before she leaves.'

Lee was relieved that not only the editor but the rest of the staff seemed quite pleased with her new appointment. They had always been a good team to work with, and she was glad that although there was some resentment because of Pat Blyth's sudden resignation under pressure, it did not rub off on her. The older woman was largely responsible for this, she realised, for she seemed only too pleased to have Lee take over some of her work immediately. Briefly she wondered who would take her own place and hoped that she would be consulted. Then she forgot herself in the work at hand, for the next issue was due at the printer's the following day.

She and Pat stayed on after the rest of the staff had gone, a not infrequent occurrence, and it was not until the last page of the printer's 'dummy' copy was completed that Lee recalled her dinner date.

She just missed one bus and had to wait twenty minutes

for another, wishing she had brought the car. She actually
owned a second-hand Volkswagen, but what with parking
problems and the energy crisis, she usually took a bus to
work and used the car only at weekends.

At the flat she made a quick cup of coffee and then
showered and pulled on a robe while she contemplated her
wardrobe. It was not particularly extensive, and she decided
with sudden dissatisfaction, not very interesting either.
What she really wanted was something light and floaty and
cool, for the day was still hot and even later in the evening
it would doubtless be a typically warm and humid summer
night.

She took out a pale grey chiffon blouse with loose, cape-
style sleeves and a cross-over bodice which she seldom
wore because the neckline seemed a little daring. Remembering Adam's mocking remark about her office clothes
she thought that he could hardly call her 'nun-like' in this!
Even though it was grey.

Laying the blouse on her bed, she pulled out a satiny
black skirt with a pattern of grey roses etched with white,
and red rosebuds scattered throughout.

She owned only one bra she could wear with the blouse
—a filmy little nothing of lace that did very little except
make the blouse not quite see-through. She didn't remember when she had last worn it, and she wasted precious
minutes before finding it tucked up deep into the back of a
bottom drawer.

Determined not to botch her make-up, she took her time
over it and then brushed her hair briefly but vigorously,
thankful that the simple style fell into place without any
fussing.

She was just stepping into her skirt when the doorbell
rang, and she called, 'Coming!' But he couldn't have heard

her, because she was still struggling with the zip, which had caught in the material and would need to be gently eased down again without tearing it, when the bell pealed again.

Hastily she pulled on the blouse and tied the sash at the waist in a hurried knot, and, holding her skirt together with her hands, went to open the door. Her face was flushed from her struggles with the zip and she hadn't yet got her shoes on. Adam looked cool and appraising.

'Come in,' she said, still clutching her skirt at the side with one hand. 'I'll only be a minute longer. Would you like a drink?' She indicated a small nineteeth-century kauri table in one corner of the lounge. 'Do you mind helping yourself?'

'Not at all,' he said, looking at the small selection of bottles on the table. 'Can I pour you something?'

'No, thanks. I won't be long.'

Lee moved towards her bedroom door and he said, 'There's no great hurry. I thought we'd take a drive first and eat when it's cooler. If that's okay with you?'

'It sounds very nice,' she said.

'Can I help at all?'

She glanced around and saw he was looking in a slightly amused way at the waistband of her skirt, and her hand holding it together. Obviously he knew something about jammed zips. He sounded very polite about it, just being helpful.

'No, thanks,' she said firmly, equally polite. 'I'll manage.'

She did, after a few minutes and a few whispered but rather unladylike words. Then she found her black high-heeled sandals and a small black satin bag into which she hastily thrust a couple of tissues, a lipstick and a comb with a little bit of money, and then she took several deep breaths and emerged looking, she hoped, cool and pretty and very much able to cope.

'I'm sorry I kept you waiting,' she said composedly, as Adam turned, glass in hand.

'Don't be sorry,' he said. 'I'm rather glad I was a little too early for you.' That was polite of him, because she knew he was dead on time. *She* was running late. 'It was worth it,' he added, smiling a little, 'to see my so efficient, calm and unflappable Miss Palmer looking for once slightly flustered.'

'Oh,' she said. 'I don't think that's very—kind.'

'But I'm not kind,' he said, and in his eyes she glimpsed something both lazy and dangerous. 'I thought you knew.'

Striving for lightness, she gave a breathy little laugh and said, 'Is that a warning?'

For a moment he was silent, looking at her almost broodingly. Then he said, 'Yes, perhaps it is. I like to play fair, you see.'

Was he playing with her? she wondered. The atmosphere suddenly seemed full of strange tension.

'Well,' she said, trying to ease it, 'I know that if I don't come up to scratch as an editor, you'll have my head.'

'As a matter of fact,' he said, downing the rest of his drink, 'it isn't your *head* that interests me tonight. At least, not alone.'

He had turned away to put down his empty glass on the corner table, and she had time to correct the surprise in her face and school it to a faint, sophisticated amusement instead.

As they left the flat he said, 'Did I tell you how lovely you look?'

'I rather gathered that you preferred me half-dressed and tousled,' she said dryly.

'Half-dressed, possibly,' he murmured, and she mentally kicked herself for wording it like that. 'But I have to admit that as you are, you're a definite asset to a man.'

'What a very chauvinistic way of putting it,' she drawled as he opened the door of a rather nice black Mazda.

'It's a compliment,' he said reprovingly, as she got in and tucked her skirt around her ankles. 'You're supposed to smile nicely and say thank you.'

'Thank you!' she said, fluttering her lashes at him.

'I have a distinct feeling you could drive a man mad, Miss cool-as-a-cucumber Palmer,' said Adam, only half-humorously. 'No trouble at all!' And he shut her door with a decided snap, before moving around to his own.

CHAPTER THREE

THEY travelled through the city and then over the bridge that spanned the narrow part of the harbour to the North Shore. It was still quite light, and there were numerous sails dotted about the water below, not only white, but red, orange, and yellow. On the Auckland side of the harbour, tall buildings seemed to float mistily at the water's edge, and by contrast as they reached the Shore side, the bridge passed right over the top of old colonial bungalows surrounded by leafy pohutukawas, oaks and pepper trees.

Adam drove smoothly and patiently, showing no signs of irritation at traffic lights or the bridge toll-gate, or even when he had to change gear behind a slow old-model car which crawled at snail-pace up the southern slope of the bridge. He conversed easily as he drove and Lee began to relax.

Once through the toll-bridge, he took the road to the East Coast Bays and eventually drove down a side road between rows of houses to a parking area near the sea.

'Feel like a walk?' he asked.

Lee nodded. Even with the windows wound down and the wind ruffling her hair, it was warm in the car, and a stroll in the fresh air would be cooling.

He took her hand to help her from her seat, and didn't relinquish it as they strolled along the grass above the beach. Children played on the sand, and one family was having a barbecue, the smell of sizzling sausages wafting to them as they passed.

31

Lee lifted her head and sniffed it pleasurably.

'Hungry?' Adam enquired, amused.

She turned her head and smiled at him. 'I can wait. This is nice.'

His fingers tightened fractionally on hers, and she looked away, because she didn't want him to know how that affected her.

'Would you like to go down on the sand?' he asked her.

Having never outgrown the childish pleasure of walking barefoot on a beach, she said immediately, 'Yes,' and added, 'But I'll have to take off my shoes.'

'Give them to me,' he said as she slipped them off, and he put one into each side pocket of his dark jacket.

He leaped lightly down the bank to the beach and when he turned to her and she made to take his hand and follow him, he put his hands firmly on her waist instead, so that she had to place hers on his shoulders as he swung her down beside him. She landed lightly, her soft breasts brushing him.

She felt his hands move down to her hips over the silky material of her skirt as he said, 'All right?' and steadied her against him.

'Yes,' she said, on a slight gasp, moving quickly away.

They walked down to firmer sand, and he said, looking at the dozen or so people in the water, 'Perhaps we should have brought swimsuits.'

'I expect the water's lovely,' she answered, and lifting her skirt a little, she moved towards the small wavelets that slid creamily up the sand, and stood ankle-deep in the water.

Watching her from a few yards back, he said, 'How is it?'

'Cold!' she answered. She turned and began to walk again, still holding her skirt up and letting the fugitive wavelets wash up over her feet when they would. Adam strolled with her, on the dry sand a few feet away, but one wave rolled a little further than the others and took him by surprise, wetting his shoes.

Lee laughed, and he reached out a long arm and grabbed her wrist, pulling her out of the water to his side, not roughly but with some force.

'*Oh!*' She looked up with some anxiety, then relaxed as she saw he was smiling. But the light in his eyes made her feel a little breathless.

'I can see you're a hoyden at heart,' he said, glinting down at her.

Feeling suddenly reckless, she smiled back at him. 'Do you mind?'

'No, I don't think I do,' he said, on a slightly odd note. 'It could be decidedly unsettling around the office, though.'

'We're not in the office,' she pointed out.

The leaping light in his eyes intensified, and, suddenly nervous, Lee eased her hand out of his grasp. 'In the office I'm a model of decorum,' she said rather quickly. 'You must have noticed.'

'I had,' he agreed, placing a light hand on her waist to steer her back towards the car. 'That's why I was planning to take you to a decorous and respectable restaurant tonight.'

'Oh, dear!' she said. 'Have I blotted my copybook?'

'Not at all. Just—surprised me a little.'

You've surprised me, too! Lee thought. Because tonight she liked him very much, quite apart from the leaping of her pulses every time he touched her. She was discovering he was very nice to be with, and relaxing too, in spite of his dynamic business personality.

Her feet were coated with sand, and she sat sideways on

the passenger seat of the car, with the door open, trying inadequately to brush it off with a tissue.

'I really need some talcum powder,' she muttered frustratedly.

Adam, who had been leaning against the side of the car and watching her futile efforts, opened the back door and brought out a leather toilet bag from the shelf at the rear of the car.

He took out a tin of male talc from it, pulled out his handkerchief from the breast-pocket of his jacket, and squatted on the grass in front of her.

'Here,' he said, 'let me do it.' His fingers closed around one ankle.

'Your suit!' she said faintly.

'Never mind!' he said almost brusquely, and shook the talc over her feet, spreading his knees so that the surplus fell on the grass between them. He wiped each foot firmly with the handkerchief, and when he had finished he shook it out, still holding one of her ankles in a warm, hard hand.

'Thank you!' she said softly, and he looked up. It was a long, unfathomable look, and she was glad that darkness was beginning at last to gather around them, because she couldn't tear her eyes away, and she didn't know what he might read in them.

He stood up and handed her her shoes, and by the time he had put away the talcum and come round into his seat and closed the door, she had put them on, and combed her hair, so that she looked sleek and tidy once more.

'Do up your safety-belt,' he reminded her, and she said, 'Oh, yes,' and fumbled with the unfamiliar catch until he leaned over and did it up for her.

'Thank you,' she said again, looking up to find he hadn't leaned back into his own seat, but was very close, his eyes on her face, dropping to her slightly parted lips.

He was going to kiss her, and she knew she was going to let him—and then the spell was broken as a party of noisy teenage boys came thumping past the car, catcalling and whistling.

Lee jerked back in her seat and Adam gave a muttered exclamation and started the engine.

They dined overlooking the harbour, at a table near huge windows that gave a fantastic view of the moon-glimmer on the dark sea, and the lights of the farther shore dipping their long reflections into the water.

The meal was served in leisurely fashion, with breaks between courses that allowed them to admire the view, talk or dance in between. From talking about *Lady* they progressed to publishing in general, and Adam held her fascinated as he told her about his four years in the United States and the publishing world there. Over crisp shrimp cocktails they discussed some of the most recent best-sellers, how they made it to the top of the lists and why they did, and agreed that sometimes the top-selling books were not particularly well written.

'But they give people what they want,' he added. 'Something larger than life—an escape from the humdrum routine that they live every day.'

Enjoying juicy carpet-bag steaks stuffed with succulent, plump oysters all the way from The Bluff at the southern tip of the South Island, they argued amicably about the role of advertising in the media. Lee was sceptical about its value, believing that it represented a colossal waste of money. 'It's all added to prices of the goods, too,' she said. 'The consumer ultimately pays for it.'

'Just as well you're an editor for *Lady*, and not on the

advertising side,' he commented. 'Don't you realise that if it wasn't for the advertising revenue, the readers would have to pay far more for the magazine?'

'Well, yes,' she admitted. 'And I suppose the same goes for newspapers and the TV. We would all be paying more for those if it wasn't for advertising.'

'You might as well face it,' he said, 'it's money that keeps the world going.'

His words struck an echo of something Brian had said just the night before. *Money makes the world go round*,' and when she had said, '*I thought it was love that did that*,' he had made some remark about Adam Broome having plenty of both.

Remembering Lisbet Carson, she pushed aside her plate and sipped at her wine constrainedly, then held the glass in both hands while she stared pensively into the lucent red liquid.

His hand came up to take it from her and place it gently back on the white tablecloth. 'What is it?' he asked, but she only shook her head, smiling.

'Come and dance with me,' he invited, standing up and taking her hand.

He danced well, holding her close but not too tightly, and when the band broke into a faster rhythm and couples swung apart and began to change to hip-swinging and foot-stamping improvisations, he did that well, too. Lee deliberately pushed aside thoughts of him dancing on other evenings with Lisbet Carson, and abandoned herself to enjoyment, laughing into his eyes when they were dancing a tantalising two feet apart, and swaying gracefully against him when the music became more dreamy and romantic.

They finished the wine and he had strawberries and cream, but she declined dessert and just had coffee before he pulled her to her feet for one last dance.

Someone dimmed the lights even further, and his left hand, that had been holding her hand close to his warm chest, left hers and slid around her waist, drawing her closer, his face against her hair.

'Lee,' he murmured. It was the first time he had said her name, and she gave a tiny shiver of pure pleasure at the sound of it. 'What is it?' he said.

She tipped back her head to look at him. 'Nothing,' she whispered.

She saw him smile a little in the near-darkness, and then his lips briefly touched hers in the lightest of kisses.

Her mouth tingled with the contact, and she let her head rest against him. One hand left her waist and began caressing her back gently, and she steadied her breathing deliberately and made her face a rigid blank as desire stirred within her body. They drew apart reluctantly as the music stopped and the lights were turned up, and he kept his hand lightly on her hip-bone as they left. She could feel the warm weight of it as she walked, and was conscious of the sinuous movement of her body against his fingers.

He drove her home rapidly and in near-silence, both hands firmly on the steering-wheel. Lee wound down the window to half-way to gain a breeze and cool her heated cheeks and body. By the time he drew the car up smoothly in front of her flat, she was almost back to normal.

She heard the click of his safety belt being undone, and fumbled with her own. His hand came over and flicked it open, and she drew hers away.

'Thank you very much,' she said. 'I had a lovely evening.'

'Then thank me properly,' he said, and reached for her, drawing her into his arms, her head tipped back against the curve of his shoulder.

'Say, "Thank you, *Adam*",' he instructed.

'You're a bully,' she whispered instead.

'I admit it,' he said with low-voiced mockery. 'Say it.' He dipped his head and trailed his lips across her thoat, and gently nipped at her skin with his teeth.

A swift surge of desire shot through her, and she gasped and wriggled in his grasp.

He lifted his head to look down at her face, illuminated faintly by a street lamp at the corner. 'Say it!' he insisted.

Lee passed the tip of her tongue over her lips and obeyed. 'Thank you, Adam.'

And then her mind echoed his name over and over again as his lips took possession of hers and stormed all her defences, making her open her mouth to him while his hands strained her body closer to his. One hand moved to rest under her armpit and press against the side of her breast. Her own right hand was pinned over his heart, and her left hand slid under his jacket and spread against his back as he made free of her mouth in a kiss that seemed to go on for ever, exploring, probing, undeniably passionate.

When he finally lifted his mouth and eased his hold a little, he held his face against her hair for an instant, then wiped his thumb firmly across her throbbing mouth, creating in her an insane desire to catch his hand and press her lips to it.

'I must go in,' she said a little desperately.

'Can I come?'

'*No!*' she said sharply, purely from an instinct for self-preservation.

His hand moved lightly over her breast and rested for a moment, hard and warm, on the deep vee of skin bared by the neckline of her blouse, before moving up to caress her throat and finally   p her chin.

'No?' he said softly, brushing her lips gently once, and then again.

'*Please don't!*' she muttered against his lips, in a tortured whisper. She turned her head from his seeking mouth. 'I don't want——'

'*You want me!*' he said with soft violence, and pulled her round to face him, his hand under her hair.

It was impossible to deny, but pride and anger came to her rescue, and she closed her lips and clenched her teeth against him when he kissed her again, straining to resist his arms.

Finally he drew away, holding her shoulders in a hard grasp. 'Do you always turn it on and off so easily, Lee?' he asked.

'Do *you* always assume a girl will invite you to stay the night if you give her dinner?' she countered swiftly.

Adam drew in a swift breath, but when he spoke his voice was steady and hard. 'I don't remember asking to stay the night.'

He hadn't, in fact, she realised. But after that kiss, she had assumed that was what he meant by his request to come in.

'Isn't that what you meant?' she asked a little shakily.

He didn't answer immediately. His hands left her shoulders and he half-turned away for a moment before his darkened gaze returned to her face. 'I'm not sure exactly what I meant,' he admitted finally. 'I just didn't want to let you go—yet. I wouldn't have asked for anything you didn't want to give.'

'But I did want to,' she said, very softly. 'That's why I said no.'

'Meaning you don't sleep around, is that it?' he asked, after a moment.

'Yes, I suppose that is what I mean,' she answered, low-voiced.

'Well, I don't exactly do that myself,' he said, abruptly. After a pause of several seconds he added, 'Shall we lunch together tomorrow?'

After a moment to adjust to his change of subject, she asked lightly, 'Business?'

'Definitely not business,' he answered firmly. 'In fact, I think we'll ban business from the table altogether. We could, for instance, concentrate on learning something about each other.'

'I'd like that,' she said simply and with sincerity.

'Good. I'll see you tomorrow, then.' He leaned over and opened her door, and watched until she had let herself into the flat before driving off.

Lee arrived at work the following morning feeling on top of the world in spite of having two late nights in a row. And in spite of the fact that it was Friday, when everyone traditionally drooped and hailed the onset of the weekend with relief.

She got through an enormous amount of work, which was as well, because she still had her own work to do as well as shouldering some of Patricia's.

'By the way,' the editor said on that subject, 'Adam wants us to discuss your replacement and make recommendations to him. I wondered about Helen. She's been showing some interest in the editorial side lately. What do you think?'

'I'd hate to lose her as a secretary, of course.' Lee smiled. 'She's so good in that job. But I think if she would like to try it, we should give her a chance—if Adam approves. She's certainly a person I can work with.'

'Well, we'll recommend her, then. Shall I tell him, or will you?'

'I will, if you like. I could go up and see him now, if he's free.'

It was only about an hour to lunchtime, and she could have mentioned it to him then, but he had said that business topics were banned, and she seemed to have been waiting an interminable time to see him again, already.

When his secretary waved her into his office, he was on the telephone. He looked up and smiled and she smiled back, but a little stiffly, because she was suddenly rather shy of him. He seemed to have resumed his business personality, and she found it difficult to believe that last night he had held her in his arms and kissed her with barely restrained passion ...

Adam put the phone down, and she realised with a shock that the coldness was back in his eyes when he looked at her and said, 'Yes, Lee? What can I do for you?'

'Pat said that you wanted us to recommend someone for my job.'

He seemed to relax a little, but she dared not do the same. She was determined now to be businesslike and efficient.

'Are you ready to make a recommendation?' he asked.

'Yes. We thought—Helen Carter.'

'Your secretary?'

'Yes. She's been working closely with both of us for over a year, and we think she could do it. We haven't mentioned it to her, but I think she might be interested. And I would like to have her.'

'If *you* want her, I'll offer her the job,' he said.

He made it sound almost as though he would have given her anything she wanted.

'Yes, well—it is important that we should be able to work well together,' she said.

'Undoubtedly.' His mouth quirked up at the corner and she relaxed a little and smiled at him again. 'We'll have to find another secretary, then.'

'Yes. Helen's so good it won't be easy to replace her.'

'Leave it to me. I'll get my secretary on to it in the morning.'

Lee stood up to go and he said, 'I'll come down to your office and fetch you at lunchtime.'

'I could meet you outside,' she offered.

'Why on earth should you do that?'

'Well—office gossip, you know.' It would be the second time.

'Tell them it's business. I have a lot to discuss with my new editor.'

They might believe it this time, but if Adam and she made a habit of lunching together, the grapevine would run positively hot. She could hardly say that to him, though, as if one lunch date was necessarily the precursor of a series.

But as she reached the door, he said gently, 'Does gossip bother you?'

Lee had been thinking of him, rather than herself, but now it occurred to her for the first time that if they *were* embarking on some sort of continuing relationship—and she realised that she hoped passionately that they were—there could be all kinds of snags and difficulties, and the entire population of the building would be watching them like a veritable flock of hawks.

'I think it might,' she said slowly. 'I do rather prefer my private life to remain private.'

'Don't worry,' he said. 'One lunch doesn't make an affair in any language. And after today, I'll be careful.'

Lee went down to her own office feeling happy and oddly cherished, but only twenty minutes later the intercom on her desk buzzed, and Adam's voice said, 'Lee?'

'Yes,' she said.

'Darling, I'm terribly sorry. Something has come up, and I have to break our lunch date.'

Her heart was reacting in such an extraordinary way to that '*darling*' that she scarcely heard the rest of the sentence.

'Lee?'

'Yes,' she said, 'it's all right. Perhaps another day . . .'

'I'll make it up to you,' he promised. 'Are you very disappointed?'

'No, of course not.'

'I was rather hoping you would be.'

Striving to make her voice behave, she said, 'You're not being very careful, are you?' She smiled teasingly as she said it, but of course he couldn't see that.

'No,' he said, after a moment. 'But I did say "after today", didn't I?'

'I'll see you later, then,' she said.

'Well—maybe not. I'm not sure how long this will take. Have a good weekend.'

'Yes,' she said. 'You, too.'

It would seem very long, but she would be busy, anyway. Maybe it would help her to get things in perspective. Because she realised that she *was* bitterly disappointed, and reacting like a besotted teenager instead of a mature and sensible young woman.

She decided not to go out for lunch at all, and asked Helen to get her some sandwiches and bring them back with her. There was plenty she could do in the lunch hour, and anything was better than sitting around brooding about her disappointment.

She worked at her desk for a few minutes, then crossed the now empty outer office to the filing cabinet by the window to extract some material she needed. She had it in her hand when she glanced out the window and saw Adam crossing the road below. She watched him because it gave her some small pleasure to do so, then she stood frozen as she saw him stretch out an arm, and Lisbet Carson detached herself from the shop doorway where she had been waiting and came into the circle of it, her hand on his shoulder as he bent his head to her face. It was a very brief kiss, and he raised his head, Lisbet laughed into his face before he turned her to walk down the street with him.

Humiliation washed in waves over Lee as she automatically shut the file drawer and walked back to her desk. She opened the file and stared at the first page for ages, not even seeing it.

Darling, he had called her, breaking their lunch date because 'something had come up'. The something being a more attractive date, of course. Why had she assumed that it was business? At least he had not exactly lied to her. If that made it any better. Perhaps it did, but not much.

What an idiot she had been, building foolish dreams on nothing more than a dinner and a kiss. She *knew* that kisses meant nothing these days. Other men had thought themselves entitled to far more than that on the strength of a dinner or two. In fact she often thought that Women's Lib had a decided point—she wouldn't have minded paying her own way and so being under no obligation, if men didn't get so peculiar about it.

She had thought that Adam was different, but reviewing the evidence it wasn't that easy to recall why.

CHAPTER FOUR

SHE was still reviewing the evidence as she drove the Volkswagen south on Saturday morning. She was a competent driver and it was a lovely morning. Normally she would have taken pleasure in the feel of the wheel responding to her hands, and the sight of the rolling green countryside passing speedily by. But today, although she determinedly tried to occupy her mind with other subjects, it kept stubbornly returning to Adam Broome—his looks, his smile, the way he had held her when they danced, and most of all the way he had kissed her so devastatingly when he took her home that night.

She remembered him saying, 'I'm not kind, I thought you knew.' And, 'I like to play fair, you see.'

He *hadn't* played fair with her. Anger took over from her other confused emotions concerning him as she remembered the caressing note in his voice as he apologised for standing her up. That had certainly been unfair, as well as unkind, and she was not going to stand for that sort of treatment from any man.

She thought of leaving her job, not knowing how she was going to be able to manage, seeing him every day. But it was unthinkable. Adam would know that it was because of him, and her pride would suffer further as a result. Besides, she did need the extra money, and doubted that she would earn as much elsewhere. The only thing to do was pretend that he meant as little to her as she obviously did to him. Which should be easy, she told herself. She was simply suffering from a temporary attraction—physical infatuation was all it amounted to, and she would surely soon recover from it. If she could just keep their relationship on a strictly business basis.

She turned off the motorway and took a country road that wound through the hills, the wild flowers spilling down grassy banks on either side of it. She would simply be cool and casual about it, she decided, and firmly but quite pleasantly refuse all future invitations that were not strictly for business purposes. Driving between wide paddocks full of sleepy cows and fat white sheep, it all seemed very simple and easy.

By the time she entered the small town of Titini, where she had been born, and changed gear as she slowed the car to fifty kilometres per hour, she felt quite relaxed and confident again. Somehow visiting home always had that effect on her.

Her brother came to the door to meet her as she parked outside the old kauri bungalow. She got out swiftly and moved up the ramp to greet him before he could come down to her, linking her arm in his so that he could unobtrusively lean on her and make his way into the living room more quickly. Her parents had married late, and although her own birth had been an unmitigated joy for them, six years later there had been difficulty with the birth of Michael. The baby had been injured, and his left side was partly paralysed. He walked with difficulty as his left foot was immobile, his left arm had little power and the fingers could not grasp. And his speech was impaired.

'You're looking good,' he said now, the impediment slightly slurring his words.

Lee smiled. 'I have good news. I'll tell you both when Mum is here.'

Her mother came in at that moment, frail-looking and rubbing her back as though it hurt. She smiled with pleasure and Lee kissed her affectionately and said, 'What have you been doing—giving yourself a backache?'

'Getting rid of a few weeds, that's all. And what have you been up to?'

Lee grinned, perching herself on the arm of an old-fashioned easy chair. 'Just getting myself promoted, that's all.' With a faint sense of burning bridges, she added, 'I'm the new editor of *Lively Lady*.'

'Darling, that's wonderful!' her mother exclaimed. 'Your father would have been proud of you!' Their father had been dead for ten years, but their mother never failed to include him in moments of family joy or crisis. She had said the same when Michael passed his university entrance examination. He was due to start at university this year, although it was going to be difficult for him both physically and financially.

Michael added his congratulations to his mother's, and Lee said, 'The best thing about it is that I get a substantial raise, too.' Turning to Michael she said, 'I'll be able to help you when you go to university, Mike. And how would you like a car of your own?'

She saw his eyes light up as he stumblingly told her how much he would like it. There was no question of his driving a normal car, and although they had sometimes discussed the possibility of his some day acquiring a specially adapted one, the price of such a luxury was until now well beyond their means.

Watching his face, and knowing how much difference it would make to her brother to have independent transport, she felt that whatever difficulties she encountered through having to work with Adam Broome would be well worth it.

The rest of the weekend passed pleasantly and busily. Lee took over the weeding that her arrival had interrupted, and found a certain therapeutic satisfaction in vigorously attacking the roots of dock and puha. Anger and hurt dissipated like magic as the garden began to look tidier and the pile of weeds in the wheelbarrow mounted.

Michael, who was busy snipping off dead branches and flowers from some shrubs with his one good hand, rescued a puha which had missed the barrow and put it on top of the rest of the weeds.

'I suppose we should cook that,' he remarked.

Lee made a face. 'I've never acquired the taste,' she said. 'To me they're just a weed.'

'You have to pick them young,' he said. 'That's what the Maoris do.'

'They're welcome to their pork and puha,' she said. 'Personally I prefer a nice carpet-bag steak.'

'Who's been feeding you carpet-bag steaks, then?' Michael asked astutely. It wasn't a dish they often whipped up at home and he was well aware that she didn't spend her time at the flat cooking gourmet meals for one.

'My new boss,' she said shortly, exasperated, to find the man cropping up in conversation. The subconscious, she decided, had a lot to answer for.

'What's he like?'

'Very much in charge,' she told him. 'A businessman to the core. Calculating, clever, and with a veneer of charm.'

Michael paused in his snipping to look over at her. 'Don't you like him?'

'It doesn't matter,' she said. 'I don't need to like the boss to do my job.'

'No, but you always said that one reason you liked working there was the fact that the other people were so nice to work with.'

'Well, I don't need to see that much of him,' she explained. 'He has other publications to attend to as well, you know.'

Michael returned to tidying up a bedraggled hydrangea. 'You know,' he said, emotion making his voice more indistinct than usual, 'I'm going to pay you back some day, for all you're doing for me.'

'Don't be silly,' Lee said lightly. 'That's what families are for.'

'Well, I want you to know Mum and I appreciate it, that's all,' he said. 'It's not much fun for her, having to wait on me the way she does. It's pretty good of you to come home practically every weekend the way you do. I'll bet you turn down lots of dates.'

'None that I miss, Michael darling. I like coming home. It refreshes me for the next week's daily grind.'

Lee did feel refreshed when she returned on Monday morning to work. Sunday had been a lazy day, and the healthy fatigue she had earned with her afternoon in the garden provided a good excuse for changing into brief shorts and a bra-top after church, and spending most of the day sunbathing on the back lawn. That had deepened her summer tan, and she donned a crisp cream shirtwaister dress with no sleeves which enhanced the golden brown of her arms and throat and felt cool and efficient.

That was just as well, because she needed all the poise she could muster, later on. She had barely got through her mail, and sent Helen to fetch some prints which were supposed to have been delivered on Friday from the photographic department, when the intercom on her desk called her attention, and Adam's voice momentarily sent her calm flying.

When he said, 'Lee? How about making up for that

lunch today?' she regained her composure and was aware of an icy anger with him which she tried to conceal. *Remember to be casual*, she told herself. She had to pretend that the whole thing had been supremely unimportant in her life.

'I'm sorry,' she said, 'I'm afraid I can't make it.'

'Tomorrow?'

'No, not tomorrow, either.'

For a long moment there was silence, and she became aware that the palms of her hands were moist with tension. Then Adam said evenly, 'Does that mean, not tomorrow— or not any day?'

'It means—not any day,' she answered. 'I'm sorry.'

'The hell you are!' he said, so softly she could hardly hear him. Then, more loudly, he added, 'I'm coming down.'

She discovered she was shaking slightly, and took a determined grip on herself. It might not be the most pleasant interview, but there was nothing to be panicky about. She might as well get it over with.

He was there in seconds, breathing a little more quickly and heavily than usual, and she guessed he had run down the stairs instead of waiting for the lift. He shut the door quietly but definitely behind him and came over to her desk where she was standing waiting for him.

'Now,' he said softly, 'what's it all about, Lee? If you're afraid of office gossip, we'll make it dinner instead of lunch, and keep it a secret, if that's what you'd prefer.'

About to say, *It isn't that*, she realised he had given her a perfect excuse that was believable in the light of their last conversation. She said instead, 'No, thank you. I'd really rather forget the whole idea.'

She was mentally marshalling arguments when he demanded irritably, 'For heaven's sake, why? If you're angry because I had to break our date last week, it's understandable, but believe me it was very important.'

'Business?' she asked, swiftly—bitterly.

'No,' he said slowly, 'not business. A friend in trouble. You see——'

'It's all right,' she said swiftly, sickened by the lie and not wanting to hear it embroidered upon. She supposed that Lisbet Carson might be counted among his friends, but she had been laughing into his face when they went down the street together. 'I told you it didn't matter,' she said. 'You've no need to make excuses to me.'

'Then if it didn't matter——'

'I just don't think it would work out,' she said. 'I told you, I like my private life to remain private. It isn't a good idea to mix business and—social life. I've been thinking it over and I decided I would prefer not to accept invitations from you unless they are—strictly business.'

He gave a soft, rueful laugh. 'I suppose I should understand that. It's exactly why I didn't rush you from the start. I've always tried to keep my own personal affairs out of the office.'

'Well then——'

'Well then—*nothing*. I changed my mind the day you walked into my office looking like Anne Boleyn—yes,' he added, at her look of puzzled astonishment, 'a siren queen. I wanted you then, and I want you now. And I'm not letting a little thing like office etiquette stand in the way. I'll deal with the gossip if and when it arises—and that's a promise, Lee.'

For a moment she almost softened, for the promise brought back an echo of the cherished feeling she had experienced when he said before that he would be careful to protect her from the grapevine. But of course he was good at that. Did Lisbet, bruised emotionally from her broken marriage, also feel cherished and protected when Adam put his arm around her and kissed her?

'I'm sure I should be flattered,' she said icily. 'But even you can't have everything you want. Maybe you could prevent the gossip, but there are other problems that arise.' For instance, she was thinking, what if he tired of her after all—if their relationship had progressed at all, would she then be able to stand going on working with him?

'I'm willing to take the risk,' he said quietly, apparently guessing at her thoughts.

'I'm not,' she said stubbornly. 'I don't want to jeopardise my job.'

He frowned at that. 'Do you mean you think I'd be petty enough to threaten your job if——'

'If you ceased to "*want*" me?' she said. 'I don't know. But things could become difficult, couldn't they?'

Her heart sank slightly as she saw his eyes and mouth harden. 'Has it occurred to you,' he asked silkily, 'that I could make things difficult for you *now*, in order to get what I want?'

It hadn't, and in truth Lee hadn't meant that she thought he would deliberately make it impossible for her to keep her job, only that there might be problems arising from a personal relationship.

'I don't think,' she answered, lifting her head a little, 'that you would be—satisfied with a woman who had to be coerced.'

'Would I have to coerce you, Lee?' he asked softly, and reached out, his hands closing on the soft skin of her upper arms and drawing her to him. She pulled against them, and clenched her fist against his hard chest, but his grip tightened and he wasn't going to let her go. Rather than start an undignified scuffle, she stared defiantly into his eyes, hoping that he read only contempt in hers.

'Shut your eyes,' he murmured, and she firmed her mouth and stubbornly shook her head. He gave a soft little laugh and his hand slid to her nape and held her while his mouth descended to her eyelids, so that she had to shut them, and then moved to her lips, unexpectedly gentle, barely touching her mouth as he teased unbearably, moving softly from her lower lip to the corner of her mouth and back again, not demanding at all but merely tantalising, until she longed desperately to relax her rigid body in his arms and part her lips and make him kiss her properly. She made a small, protesting sound, and his lips firmed on hers, still gentle but taking her mouth fully now. With a supreme effort of will she remained unyielding and stiff against his embrace.

There was a soft tap on the door, and she pushed against him in panic—unnecessarily, because he had heard it too and had already loosened his hold on her. She caught at the back of her chair to steady herself, and Adam stepped back quickly. So that when Helen entered the room, clutching a file of photographs, they were several feet apart.

'Oh, I'm sorry,' she said. 'I didn't realise you were here, Mr Broome.'

'It's all right, Helen,' said Lee. 'Thanks for fetching the photos.' She reached out and took them from the girl with a smile, and put the file on her desk.

When Helen had left the room and closed the door, there was for several seconds a tense silence. Adam hadn't moved, and Lee stared unseeingly at her desk, wondering if she had betrayed herself before the secretary's unwitting intervention.

When she thought she could control her expression, she

looked up at him, and said coolly, 'I think that rather proves my point, doesn't it? There are just too many complications. And,' she added for emphasis, 'I just don't want *you* enough to make it worthwhile.'

She knew immediately that she should not have said that. It was unnecessary and bordered on insulting. But retribution was swift and brutal.

'Perhaps you're right, after all,' Adam said curtly. 'Cold little cats sometimes make very good businesswomen—if I have to make a choice, I think I prefer to have you in my business rather than in my bed. At least you're competent —here.'

He left her gasping with inexpressible rage and humiliation. If she had been moved to regret her last remark, his effectively cancelled out any need for compunction. His weapons were infinitely more dangerous and wounding than hers. It was no ambition of hers to be 'good in bed' and certainly she had never had any particular intention of sharing his, but to be told that he doubted her ability in that direction—in such a deliberately beastly way—was, perhaps illogically, a painful blow to her self-esteem. For the rest of the morning, while part of her brain dealt with planning the following week's issue of the magazine, the rest of it buzzed with angry retaliations she might have made to Adam's deadly gibe.

If she had ever seriously thought that Adam might use his position against her, she would have been reassured over the next week or so. He treated her with normal courtesy and complimented her on her work when he felt it was specially good, just as he always had. They practically never saw each other alone and she doubted that anyone else realised that each time they were in the same room there was an undercurrent of tension and hostility and something less easy to define that stretched between them like a fine hot wire. Every time he left the room she felt herself gradually relax as the tension that had built up drained from her. She would, she told herself, she *must* get over it. She needed only time.

Sometimes she doubted that Adam felt the strain of their relationship at all, he seemed so aloof and urbane, but just occasionally when he looked at her there was a flicker of awareness in his eyes, and she would remember him telling her that he wanted her. She supposed he had meant that in a physical sense, and she deliberately fed the resentment that stirred in her at the memory, because he had never had any right to suppose she was 'available' in that sense, and anger was a defence against the unwanted but undeniable attraction that he had for her. All the same, no matter how she attempted to suppress it, the faint flicker of desire in his eyes never failed to stir an answering response in her, and there was some bitter satisfaction in knowing that although she had refused him, and although she might not be the only woman who could stir that spark in him, he wanted her still.

In desperation one night she went out with Brian Small again, dancing at a new nightclub that had opened in the city. She let him hold her close as they circled the dimly lit floor, and sparkled gaily for him, trying to force her own enjoyment. When he took her home she invited him in for coffee and let him take her in his arms and kiss her before he left. Always before she had allowed him only a fairly perfunctory goodnight kiss, and his acceptance of that was one of the reasons why she continued to see him. She had never had to fight him off or talk him into leaving at a reasonable hour, and the phrase 'just good friends' was one that might easily have applied to them.

Tonight she didn't pull away from him, but instead

kissed him back and didn't stop him when he kissed her again, more deeply. But although she tried to respond, she found herself growing less eager as his breathing quickened and his hands became more urgent.

When he had gone, she undressed and scrubbed herself under the shower before going to bed. Obviously it was going to do no good trying to find in another man's arms what her body contrarily felt only in Adam's, no matter that she liked Brian as a person a whole lot better. She had simply made herself feel cheap and dishonest, and she had probably ruined a perfectly good friendship as well.

'Damn Adam Broome!' she muttered to herself in the darkness, thumping her fists into her pillow in frustrated rage. She *must* get over this mad obsession soon!

CHAPTER FIVE

UNIVERSITY enrolments were opening, and when Lee went home at the weekend, she brought Michael back with her. On Monday morning she drove him to the university. There seemed to be nowhere to park, and she had to let him off at the main door and then drive around trying to find somewhere to put the car. Stairs were difficult for him, and although he hated needing help, she knew he would rather she gave it than that he should have to appeal to a passing stranger.

By the time she had helped him up the stairs and finally accepted his impatient assurances that he would manage now, she was very late. It didn't help to find a parking ticket on the window of the car when she finally rushed back to it. It *had* been parked illegally on a yellow line, but really there had been nowhere else to put it.

She flew past Helen and into her office feeling hot and guilty, to find Adam Broome leaning against her desk, reading a typescript. He looked as though he had been there for ages.

'Oh—are you waiting for me?' she asked in some confusion. 'I'm sorry I'm late. I had to bring the car this morning to give someone a lift, and the parking——'

'Stop making excuses, Lee,' he said curtly. 'You're not a junior typist, and I'm well aware that you spend half your lunch hours working. You're perfectly entitled to be a few minutes late now and then. Who wrote this?'

She closed the door of the cupboard on her bag and

smoothed her hair, then crossed the room to see the type-written sheets that he was holding.

When she saw what it was, she instinctively snatched it from his hand, exclaiming, 'That's private! Where did you get it?'

'It was lying on your desk,' he answered. 'I assumed it was something you were considering for publication in *Lively Lady*.'

'It isn't,' she said shortly, opening a drawer and sliding the typescript into it. 'I thought I'd put it in a drawer yesterday.'

'It was on the desk,' he said again. 'Are you accusing me of going through the drawers?'

'No, of course not!' But her manner had been hostile and she tried to temper it. 'What did you want?'

'Later,' he said impatiently. 'Just now, I want to know who wrote that piece on women and leadership, and why you're not printing it.'

'It isn't the sort of thing our readers go for,' she said.

'Rubbish! I thought we agreed that they were ready for something different. It's lively and well-written and thought-provoking material, and just the sort of thing I'd like to see you try out in *Lady*.' He paused. '*You* wrote it, didn't you?'

'Yes,' she admitted. 'But not for *Lady*.'

'Are you working for another magazine on the side?'

'Of course not. I do a bit of freelance writing, though.'

'What were you going to do with it, then?'

'See if I can sell it,' she told him.

'To another publication?'

'Yes!'

'I might call that disloyal.'

Lee stared at him. 'But we've never used that sort of

thing. I don't use my own name,' she added.

'How much have you had published?' he asked curiously.

She shrugged. 'Quite a lot.'

'I'd like to see some of it. And I want to see more of "that sort of thing" in *Lady*. I know you've been gradually introducing new subjects and approaches, but so far the sales have remained static.'

'We've only had a few weeks——' she began to protest.

'Long enough for a trend to show,' he said. 'I don't think that your gradual change is going to get results. That's what I really wanted to see you about. I'm meeting with an advertising expert today, and I want you there too.'

'When?'

'This afternoon. Two o'clock, in my office.'

'I'll be there,' she promised, inexplicably hurt that he had arranged this without consulting her.

'See that you are.' He moved towards the door, and she made a childish grimace as it closed behind him.

Lee found the meeting mentally exhausting. Not at all sure that she liked the idea in the first place—it was directly against her own advice to Adam—Lee tried to overcome her prejudice and be constructive. The two men seemed to bounce ideas off each other in a fast-paced, high-powered discussion, and she found her own role was mainly to supply information.

When the other man had gone she sat on in Adam's office, feeling decidedly wrung, her head reeling with talk of full-page newspaper spreads, television spots, competitive gimmicks and the whole gamut of a projected intensive advertising campaign. She was also slightly nervous because there had been some suggestion that as the new editor she might be 'presented as a personality,' whatever that meant, and although she had vetoed the idea, and the conversation passed to something else, she had an odd feeling that her protest had not been taken seriously.

As Adam returned to his chair, looking vitally alive and stimulated, she asked sourly, 'Are we going to re-name the magazine *New Lady*?'

He looked at her sharply, registering the irony in her tone. But he said slowly, 'Actually, it's an idea. I quite like that.'

'You're welcome to it,' she said smartly.

His eyes narrowed slightly. 'I know you don't like the idea of a new-style magazine with an appropriate fanfare for the launching,' he said. 'But in case you hadn't noticed, you've been overruled. I'm expecting your full co-operation.'

'You'll have it,' she assured him coldly. 'You did once tell me that at least I knew my job.'

A slightly cruel smile edged his mouth for an instant. 'As I recall, you were being fairly free with—compliments, yourself.'

Oh, but I'm not a patch on you, she assured him silently, watching his cold blue eyes. Antagonism raced along every nerve, and she stood up, wanting to leave him quickly before he noticed how deeply he affected her. The only way to win against this man was to make sure he thought her completely indifferent to him, neither loving nor hating.

'Just a moment,' he said, pulling a chequebook out of the drawer of his desk and scribbling hastily in it.

'I want you to choose a present for Pat Blyth,' he explained. 'You probably know her better than anyone else on the staff.' Tearing off the cheque and handing it to her, he said, 'You should be able to get her something decent with that.'

Looking at it, Lee thought so too. Aloud, she said, 'A golden handshake, they call it. Shall I buy her a watch? I should say you'd get a very handsome one for this sort of money.'

'If you think she'd like a watch, get one by all means,' he said evenly.

'I think she needs a job more,' said Lee, uncharacteristically responding to his control with recklessness.

His breath hissed between his teeth. 'I'm not going through that again, Lee. *The subject is closed.*'

'With this?' she asked tauntingly, waving the cheque. 'You think money will solve everything, don't you? This won't find Pat another job—have you any idea how difficult it will be at her age? This job has been her whole life, you know—she never married.'

'Oh, spare me!' he said irritably. 'I daresay she has a widowed mother and a crippled brother to support, too, and I'm taking bread from their mouths!'

That momentarily stunned her. She could have said, 'No, but I have,' but she was so jolted no retort occurred to her; she thought he was baiting her deliberately. Then she realised that of course he wasn't. He knew nothing about her family, and if he had he would never have made a crass remark like that. It had never entered her head that their situation was a cliché, the stuff of which bad jokes were made, but of course it was. Not that she was the sole support of her mother and brother, but her salary was pretty vital.

At her wordless stare, Adam went on with some exasperation, 'Look, I don't *enjoy* doing these things. I gave the woman every chance. I'm running a business here,' he added in a harder voice, 'not a benevolent home.'

'Oh, that's certainly true!' she agreed, recovering herself and giving him a brittle smile.

With a muffled exclamation, he came striding round the desk. Lee's instinct was to run, but she tipped up her head instead and faced him as he stopped in front of her. She could see he was in an icy rage, but he didn't touch her.

'One day——' he muttered, and then stopped, his teeth clenching sharply on the words.

Then he reached out a long arm to the door and opened it for her, almost as though he couldn't quite trust himself to keep his hands off her.

As Lee walked past him, her eyes firmly fixed straight ahead, into the outer office, she couldn't help wondering if his impulse had been to shake her or to kiss her. Either way, she was sure it would have been a fairly violent affair.

She was quite unable to repress a faint quiver of excitement at the thought.

She was relieved to find on her return to her flat that evening that Michael had found his way safely there. He hated to be coddled, and she knew from experience that he could manage most situations, but a vague worry about him had been in the back of her mind all day. She was pleased to see him looking happy and rather proud of himself. He followed her into the tiny kitchen and pretended to be making himself useful while he told her all about his day.

'Do you remember Mark Gould?' he asked as she gave him a gentle shove away from the refrigerator so that she could take out some eggs and sliced ham to make an omelette.

'From Titini?' she asked. 'He was at school with me. Of course I remember him. I had a quite a crush on him, once. He moved after leaving school.'

'That's right. He's been truck-driving for some time. Came to Auckland to work, but now he's left his job and wants to get a degree—the same course that I'm doing, actually.'

'I take it that you met him today?'

'Yes, he seemed quite pleased to see me. I think he had an ulterior motive, though.' As Lee glanced up questioningly, he gave her his lopsided grin that she always found rather endearing, although she naturally never told him so. 'He said he remembered you,' Michael added. 'And that you were one of the prettiest girls in his class at school.'

Lee made a small sound of disbelief. 'As I remember, the only girl he had eyes for at the time was Sheila Prince—she had long black hair and a fantastic skin, when the rest of us were either freckled or spotty.'

'Well, spotty or not, he wants to meet you again. He's going to pick me up tomorrow—we both have some books to buy.'

'Mark has a car?'

'You bet! A pretty fabulous Mercedes. He gave me a lift home in it. He's not your ordinary run-of-the-mill student, you know. Truck-driving pays quite well.'

'But he's giving it up to go to university and get a degree?'

'That's right. If you ask me, he's quite a guy.'

He certainly sounded like it, Lee had to agree. Remembering him as a tall, dark-haired, good-looking boy, she was curious to see what sort of man he had become.

As far as looks went, she found out the following morning, for he came early, saying that there would be crowds of people in the university bookshop later in the morning.

Lee opened the door to him, and for a few moments they assessed each other with mutual curiosity. Of course he had filled out, his shoulders were broader, his face more mature. She hadn't remembered his eyes, but they were brown and at the moment full of warm approval.

'You look great,' he said. 'Prettier than ever.'

'Come in, Mark.' She opened the door wide. 'Michael's in the bathroom. He won't be long.'

He sat down on the long sofa that opened into a bed for Michael at night, and smiled at her. She found herself comparing the smile with Adam Broome's and mentally kicked herself for it. She gave Mark a warm smile of her own in return and said, 'It's nice of you to give Michael a lift. We're hoping to get him a special car soon, but in the meantime transport for him means other people's cars— buses are awkward.'

'He tells me he'll be living with you for a while. My place is not far from here. I can pick him up every day when term begins, if you'd both like that.'

'I wasn't hinting,' she said hastily. 'I have a car, and we had arranged that I could drop him off on my way to work each day.'

'I didn't think that you were,' he said. 'But it's no trouble for me. I'm passing anyway, and it would save you going out of your way. Also, as we're going to be doing the same course, anyway, I don't mind giving Mike a hand now and then over stairs and doors. He doesn't find them easy, does he?'

'It's awfully good of you——' she began.

'Don't be silly. I've always admired guts, and young Mike has plenty, doesn't he? I can remember seeing him back home in Titini, when he was just a little bloke, struggling to keep up with the other kids in some game or other.'

'Yes, he would,' she said. 'He's going to have a struggle now, too. Not mentally—he's clever. But physically it will be hard for him. He'll need friends.'

'He's got one.'

Lee was very glad of that, and would have told him so if Michael had not limped into the room at that moment, apologising for keeping Mark waiting.

'Don't worry,' Mark replied as he stood up. 'I've been going over old times with your sister. Only we didn't have long enough. We must really get together some time, Lee. How about it?' he asked.

'Why not tonight?' she asked him. 'Come and eat with us. I make great Wiener Schnitzel.'

'Thanks!' He sounded delighted. 'I'll take you up on that.'

'Six-thirtyish, then?'

'Fine. I take it you drive yourself to work?'

'Usually I take a bus. It saves hassles with traffic—and conserves petrol.'

'I'll drop you off,'—and in spite of her mild protest that it was taking him out of his way, he persuaded her to accept a ride.

He let her off at the office door, stopping in a No Parking area to do so, and Lee stood on the pavement and waved as the Mercedes moved away into the stream of traffic again.

She was smiling as she walked into the building and ran for the lift, which Helen was holding for her, having evidently just arrived also.

'Thanks!' said Lee as the door shut them in and the lift began to rise. 'I'd hate to arrive late again, after yesterday.'

Helen smiled in sympathy. 'Did Mr Broome haul you over the carpet yesterday? It was bad luck that he happened to be waiting for you, especially as you're hardly ever late.'

'No,' Lee said hastily. 'He was very nice about it, actually.'

'He isn't so bad to work for, really, is he?' Helen mused as the lift halted and they walked out on to their floor. 'Remember how we all dreaded his coming?'

'I remember how *you* did,' said Lee, thinking that she might have dreaded it herself if she had known what effect Adam Broome was going to have on her.

'I'd like to get away on time after work,' she added, stopping by Helen's desk. 'There aren't likely to be any hitches today, are there?'

'Shouldn't think so,' Helen assured her. Then, with a smile, she asked, 'Anything to do with the guy in the big Merc that brought you to work?'

'Something,' Lee admitted with amusement. 'He's coming to dinner tonight, and I have to buy some veal on the way home for schnitzel. I've promised him a taste of my best cooking.'

'Is he special?'

Lee laughed. The other girl's interest was friendly rather than nosey, and she didn't mind it. 'He's an old friend from my home town,' she said. 'I hadn't seen him in years until this morning. But he's nice,' she added, remembering his care for her brother, which made her think of him with warmth. 'I always thought so, and he hasn't changed.'

'And good-looking,' Helen commented. 'I caught a glimpse of him when he let you off. Who was——'

Lee presumed she was about to ask who was the other passenger in the car, but they were interrupted by a sarcastic male voice, instantly recognisable as Adam's, as he emerged from Lee's office.

'Sorry to break up the girlish confidences,' he said, 'but I'd like a word with you, if you don't mind, Lee.'

Helen gasped and murmured something that was quite incoherent, and Lee swept into her office without a word, her cheeks burning faintly.

She dumped her bag on her desk and swung to face him as he shut the door.

'It's only five minutes to nine,' she pointed out.

'Then if you insist, I'll wait until nine o'clock before I begin talking business,' he said with a dangerous glint in his eyes. 'What would you suggest we do to occupy the time meanwhile?'

'I didn't mean that,' she said. 'I was just pointing out that you had no need to imply that Helen and I were wasting time chatting in the firm's time.'

'I wasn't aware that I had.'

'Well, I don't know what else you'd call it,' she retorted almost sulkily. 'Bounding out of my office with snide remarks about "girlish confidences". Were you checking up in case I was late again?'

'Don't be stupid! I suppose it's too much for you to accept that I came "bounding out" as you call it, because I was an unwitting eavesdropper on a conversation that obviously was supposed to be private. I thought I'd better let you know I was here before you began to get too confiding.'

Adam looked rather fed up, and realising that he might be in the right, she said, 'I'm sorry.' Then she added, 'And I've never thought you were dishonest.'

His mouth twisted and he said sardonically, 'Only devious—is that it?'

'I've never suggested anything of the sort!' Lee snapped.

'No—only thought it.'

Angrily, she said, 'I can't help what I think—and how would you know, anyway?'

'My dear girl, I told you the very first time I saw you. Your face is remarkably expressive, when you forget to guard it.'

'*Don't call me that!*'

Adam looked faintly surprised at her vehemence. Then he laughed softly. 'Why? Because you're not? But I thought I'd made it quite clear that you could be.'

'And *I* thought I'd made it quite clear that I don't want to be,' she replied.

'I live in the hope that I can change your mind,' he said mockingly.

'Then you've changed yours,' she said shortly. 'I thought you had quite decided you preferred me to stick to business.'

'Don't you recognise pique when you see it?' he asked. 'No man likes to be told that the woman he wants doesn't want him. Even if he knows it isn't true.'

She had been unprepared for that challenge, for the knowing confidence in his eyes when he made it. But she met it bravely.

'I might have been attracted to you for a little while,' she said coolly. 'But it didn't last.' She gave a small shrug and said, 'I'm sorry!' and made to turn away, to her desk.

His hand was hard on her arm, forcing her to face him. '*Attracted?*' he repeated sarcastically. 'You *wanted* me, Lee —you damned well admitted it!' He gripped her other arm as she tried to strain away from his hand, holding her so tightly that it hurt. His eyes, intensely blue and glittering, raked her face and body and returned to the mouth that she had firmed in stubborn anger, suppressing the other emotions that leaped through her at his touch and the nearness of him. His voice low and seductive, he said, 'I remember how you responded to me, Lee—the feel of your mouth, its softness, the way your lips parted for me. I remember your heart beating against my hand, your hands touching me ...'

She remembered too, and her remembering body yearned to repeat the experience, but she also remembered his saying, 'Darling, something's come up ...' and Lisbet Carson laughing as she walked into his arms.

'I had a lot of wine that night,' she said.

His grip suddenly tightened unbearably as he jerked her closer, and she was unable to suppress a wincing gasp of pain.

He released her immediately, and she refrained with an effort from rubbing her arms with her hands. She glanced down, following his gaze, and saw the marks of his fingers as white streaks against her tan, that were turning to a faint red.

'I didn't mean to hurt you,' he said. 'You're the only woman I know who could easily provoke me to violence.'

'Not intentionally,' she told him. 'I'd really much prefer to have nothing more to do with you!'

'Unfortunately,' he drawled, 'unless you're planning to resign, you'll just have to put up with me.'

'Unfortunately,' she echoed sarcastically, 'I need the money. But I don't think that putting up with being assaulted by you is part of my job.'

Surprisingly, a faint tinge of colour showed on his cheekbones. 'It isn't. But I think I could justly plead provocation. I promise to put a curb on my temper if you'll do the same for your tongue.'

Lee was silent, knowing that with him she did say things she would normally not have said to her managing editor. She found it extraordinarily difficult, sometimes, to remember their relative positions.

Apparently taking her silence for consent, he moved to the door. 'By the way,' he said, turning with his fingers on the handle, 'I really came down to tell you to take the afternoon off to buy that present for Pat Blyth. You'll have time to do your own shopping as well. I hope your—friend enjoys his meal.'

Lee didn't answer that. She sat down and began with

great energy to rearrange her desk, wrenching her mind with some effort to the day's work, and sorting mentally what she could delegate so as to leave a few hours early without having it pile up for tomorrow. She kept her mind so busy that she hardly had time to wonder why Adam had bothered to wait around to tell her in person that trivial little message that he could easily have conveyed via the office intercom system, or even through his secretary.

CHAPTER SIX

LEE didn't buy a watch for Pat, but a silver tea service on a matching tray. Then she bought some veal and fresh vegetables and hurried back to the flat to cook dinner.

Mark arrived promptly at six-thirty, and over a leisurely drink the three of them talked about old times, recalling incidents and people from their childhood. Mark admitted that he had not seen Titini for years, and seemed interested to hear of the changes which had taken place since he left it. Lee was pleased to see Michael, who was often shy and self-conscious in company, taking an animated part in the conversation.

The schnitzel was cooked to perfection, and Mark was sincere in his appreciation. 'I'm not a bad cook myself,' he said. 'Living alone, I had to learn to survive—but I'm not in your class, Lee.'

Lee smiled acknowledgement of the compliment as she served the sweet, a pineapple and whipped-cream concoction which earned more praise from both men.

'Have you always lived alone?' she asked Mark.

'At first I dossed in hostels,' he answered. 'Then I used to have a flat-mate. When he got married, I didn't bother to find anyone to replace him. There are advantages to living alone.'

'Yes,' Lee agreed, and in case Michael should think she would rather he didn't stay with her while attending university, she added hastily, 'It can get lonely, though.'

With an amused little smile Mark said, 'I can usually find

71

company when I want it.' His eyes held Lee's as he said it, with a hint of teasing invitation, and Michael looked from one to the other of them with slightly raised brows.

'You have the best of both worlds, then,' Lee said steadily. 'Lucky you.' Then she swiftly changed the subject to the day's newspaper headlines. It was flattering to know that Mark was interested in her. He was a good-looking man and seemed pleasant company, but she didn't want to be rushed into anything. Looking at him covertly later as he sat drinking coffee and talking to Michael, she thought that Mark might easily be an antidote to Adam Broome's disturbing effect on her. He had all the necessary qualifications, including a quality of kindness that seemed entirely lacking in Adam.

Patricia Blyth's farewell drew a number of people from other departments in the building, and the outer office was full when Adam Broome himself presented the silver tea-service to her, making a short but graceful speech of appreciation for her many years' work on *Lively Lady*.

The assembled staff put down their glasses of champagne —also provided by the management—and clapped enthusiastically as Patricia accepted with a brief speech of her own, barely suppressed tears making her voice unsteady. Lee, standing beside Brian Small, felt her own eyes prickling in sympathy.

'Putting a brave face on it, isn't she?' Brian whispered in her ear. 'The boss looks pleased with himself, though.'

Lee looked at the small group of executives just behind Patricia, to see Adam smiling at something that one of the others was saying to him. For an instant, as though he had somehow guessed she was looking at him, his eyes met hers across the room, then he stepped forward to take

Patricia's arm and lead her to a chair, as the applause died and someone started a chorus of 'For she's a jolly good fellow.'

She said a private goodbye to Pat later, in the editor's office.

'It's all yours, now, Lee,' said Pat, stuffing the last of her few personal odds and ends into a capacious handbag.

'I shall miss you,' sighed Lee.

'Oh, nonsense,' was the brisk reply. 'You've been doing most of the job for weeks. You'll make a splendid job of it.'

Smiling faintly at Pat's preoccupation, even now, with the magazine, Lee said gently, 'I meant personally.'

'Oh.' The older woman looked both confused and pleased. 'That's nice of you, Lee. I'd like to—keep in touch.'

'So would I. Are you definitely going on that cruise that you talked about?'

'Definitely. It's all booked for next week.'

'Then contact me when you get back, won't you? We'll get together over a meal.'

'Thank you. Well——' Pat glanced around the small room, 'this is it.' She bent to pick up the large carton that held the silver tea service. 'You must come and have tea with me,' she smiled. 'We'll play ladies and use my lovely parting gift. Adam told me that you chose it.' Hampered by her bag and a file which she held, as well as a jacket, she held the carton awkwardly.

Lee took the box from her as she straightened. 'I'd love that. I'll carry this to your car.'

After the box was carefully stowed away in the back seat of Pat's Mini, Lee stood back and waved as the small car made its way out of the company car park. She slowly retraced her steps to the office, and stood in the doorway, struck by the desolate air of the neatly cleared desk, and the mute pathos of one half-open, empty drawer.

Everyone else had gone home, and the outer office was also deserted, but scattered papers here and there and desk-tops cluttered with pencils and other paraphernalia testified that the occupants would return to work in the morning.

Lee wandered into her own office, feeling oddly depressed. She took out her bag and combed her hair, and made to walk briskly past the door of the empty room.

Then she paused, and going to the telephone on her desk, picked it up and dialled her own number. Michael answered, and she told him she would be late home. He accepted the news cheerfully and said he would open a tin of baked beans and have them on toast.

'Keep some for me,' she said, before ringing off. Then she put down her bag and went to work.

An hour and a half later, she had transferred everything from her old room to the editor's office, collecting a good-sized paper bag full of rubbish on the way. Her depression had disappeared, and her new premises looked businesslike and ready for use.

She was contemplating her kumara plant and wondering how to remove its trailing tendrils intact from its half-dozen tacks in the wall, when Adam's voice said from the doorway, 'Need any help?'

'*Oh!* You scared me!' she exclaimed, whirling round.

'Sorry. Actually, *you* surprised me. When I saw the lights, I expected to find Pat here.'

'She left ages ago.'

'Good. I was afraid I might find her weeping into a left-over glass of champagne.'

'She's probably doing that at home.'

'Perhaps.' He sounded quite indifferent.

'It doesn't bother you at all, does it?'

'Would you believe me if I said it did?'

Looking at the hard mockery in his face, she said flatly, 'No.'

Adam shrugged and looked around the room. 'I see you're losing no time, anyway,' he commented, rather nastily. 'I take it that's all your stuff in Pat's—the editor's office?'

'That's right,' she said tightly. 'I don't want to be wasting time in the morning.'

'Of course.' His voice was gentle, but she was sure the mockery was still there.

Turning from him, she began to carefully lift trailing vines from the wall. For a few moments Adam watched in silence, and then as she made to take the pot from its hanging bracket, he said quietly, 'Let me.'

The pot safely in his hands, while she gathered up the slender trails of green, he said, 'I take it this goes next door, too?'

'Please.'

She walked beside him, and he placed it on the desk in the other room.

'Now what?' he asked. 'Do you have a screwdriver to get that bracket out and shift it to here?'

Lee opened a drawer and took out a small plastic pack and extracted a tiny screwdriver. She didn't offer it to him, and was half expecting that he would make a move to take it from her, but he didn't.

Lee walked back to her former office and deftly removed the screw from the bracket. When she returned, Adam was lounging against the desk, his arms folded in front of him.

He watched as she positioned the screw, doffed one shoe and tapped the head of the screw smartly a few times before driving it into the wall with the little screwdriver. As she turned and replaced the shoe on her foot, he was laughing softly.

'Feminine ingenuity!' he grinned, carefully gathering up the pot and its contents and helping her hang it on the bracket. Lee retrieved the drawing pins and soon had the plant looking quite at home, the green leaves gracefully trailing across the wall beside the desk.

'Very effective,' commented Adam, surveying the result with a critical eye. His gaze returning to her face, he asked, 'I suppose you haven't eaten, have you?'

Lee shook her head. 'I'll get something at home. I'm going now.'

'Why don't we go somewhere and eat together?' he suggested. 'I'm starving, myself.'

Lee hesitated and he said dryly, 'Strictly platonic, Lee. It was just a friendly invitation—I don't feel like eating alone.'

Knowing she should refuse, she said, 'All right, then. Thank you.'

The restaurant was small and intimate, but Adam seemed determined to keep to his word, making lightly friendly conversation as they ate.

She should have been relieved, but instead found herself faintly piqued by it. Even while she responded with polite platitudes of her own, she felt resentful of the coolly impersonal look in his eyes, the calmly urbane manner he had assumed.

Some instinct within her reacted without her even realising it. Her smiles became more provocative, her every gesture more feminine.

The only effect that she could see was that he became

even more remote, perhaps faintly bored. It shouldn't have mattered, of course, but it did, and Lee felt both hurt and angry. She fell silent, staring into her empty coffee cup as he finished his, her mouth unconsciously assuming a sulky look.

'Ready?' he asked, and she looked up to find him watching her with a hint of speculation. She nodded and he paid the bill and stood up.

'I'll take you home,' Adam said.

'There's no need——' she began, but he interrupted with a note of impatience.

'Let's not argue, Lee. It would spoil a pleasant evening.'

Would it? she wondered, feeling suddenly depressed. It didn't seem to her to have been particularly pleasant. It was true that they hadn't quarrelled, but the whole episode seemed to have been an exercise in superficiality. There had been some invisible barrier between them, so that although they could see and speak to each other, no real communication had taken place.

Adam drove her home in almost total silence, gliding expertly to a smooth halt outside the flat.

'Thank you for the dinner,' she said. 'It was delicious.'

'Thank you for the company,' he returned. 'It was—delectable.'

The irony in his tone made her turn her head quickly to look at him. In the light from a street lamp she could see him smiling in a slightly cynical fashion. Uneasily, she made to move away, her hand fumbling for the handle of the door.

A hand shot out and grasped her wrist, pulling her round again to face him in the dim light. 'You flirt quite beautifully, Lee,' Adam said softly.

Lee shook her head in passionate denial. 'I wasn't flirting! I was merely trying to be pleasant company—to show some friendly appreciation——'

'Then show some now——' he muttered harshly, his arm going round her shoulders to pull her close to him. His mouth was hard and warm on her, punitive rather than passionate, almost hurtful in its leashed violence. She tried to push him away, making a small protesting sound in her throat. As though to capture it, his mouth left hers and fell to the base of her throat in a fierce caress.

Her senses clamoured with the sweet shock of it, and her anguished, 'No!' came out as little more than a whispered moan.

His head lifted and he looked down at her face, his eyes shadowed with the light behind him. 'You've wanted this,' he said huskily. 'Why else have you spent the last hour trying to captivate me?'

'I didn't!' she said tensely. 'I *didn't* want this! I *don't* want you, Adam,' she added more strongly, fear of betraying herself making her more adamant.

'Then what game are you playing with me, Lee? Do you enjoy leading a man on and then leaving him high and dry? You can't deny that tonight you've invited me to think you would welcome my kisses.'

'That's not true!' she gasped, unbearably hurt by his words. 'You're only saying it because you're angry.'

'*Yes*, I'm angry. It was you who wanted to keep our relationship strictly ice-cool. That's how I tried to play it tonight, but you've been coming on like a——'

'*Don't!* Please, Adam, stop it!' She managed to free one hand and pushed strongly against his chest, putting a little distance between them, although her wrist was still captive in his implacable hold.

'Damn you, Lee, it's true and you must know it!'

Helplessly, she shook her head, putting her free hand up to her eyes in a futile attempt to shield herself from his angry contempt.

'I *don't* know!' she said. 'I don't know.' Remembering that she had been resentful of his cold attitude, she wondered if he might be right, and was shamed by the implication. 'Maybe there is some truth in it,' she admitted. 'But I didn't mean it that way. I'm sorry if you—misunderstood.'

He dragged her hand away, saying roughly, 'Look at me!'

Slowly she raised her eyes to his, mutely appealing for his understanding.

Adam muttered some exclamation under his breath, and his hands left hers and grasped her hair, tipping back her head as he stared into her face. In a low voice, he said, 'I ought to kiss you until you cry for mercy ... and then keep on kissing you until you've no breath left to cry ... are you telling me you didn't know what you were doing?'

'Yes. Adam, *please*—let me go!'

His hands moved again to cup her face between them, his touch suddenly gentle.

Lee closed her eyes, wondering how she would stand it if he kissed her again. She felt she might almost melt under his hands, and if he was going to be gentle with her, she was capable of any mindless folly.

Then his hands were gone, and a cold breath of air made her shiver as he opened the car door and then leaned back in his seat.

'Get out, Lee.' His voice sounded suddenly weary. 'I suppose it just isn't possible for us to be friends. In future we'd better stick strictly to business.'

'Yes,' she said, sliding out. 'I'll see you in the morning.'

Adam gave an impatient exclamation, slammed the door and drove away.

Lee didn't see Adam the next day, however, nor for several days. She should have been glad of that, she supposed, for he invariably disturbed her peace of mind in one way or another. Instead she felt oddly depressed. It seemed he was deliberately keeping out of her way.

With the full responsibility for the magazine now, she was kept well occupied, and the other members of the staff were enthusiastic about the changes she was making. There was to be a special edition combined with the advertising campaign to launch the new-style *Lively Lady*, and as well as working on the current issue and tentatively assigning pieces to other future ones, Lee and her new assistant were looking for the cream of their current crop to ensure that the special edition would be a winner. Lee added an extra 'in' tray to those already on her desk to contain material being considered for it.

'What do you think of this, Lee?' Helen asked one morning, handing her a bulky manuscript.

Lee glanced at the title and raised her eyebrows. 'What do *you* think of it?' she asked in her turn.

'Well, as you can see, it deals with sexuality, and it's fairly frank. It's based on research and well written.' She grinned, and added, 'Miss Blyth would never have considered it, but with our new image, I thought *you* might.'

Lee smiled back. 'Maybe. I'll have a look at it later.'

Her desk phone called her attention, and Marion Myers, their new secretary, informed her that Brian Small was on the line.

As Helen slipped out of the room, Lee rather reluctantly spoke to him. She had been out with Brian once since the night she had shamed herself by allowing him to kiss her much too ardently, and it had taken a good deal of tact to prevent a repeat performance.

To two more invitations she had pleaded pressure of work and put him off. He had accepted that with good grace, but she knew she could not procrastinate for ever.

In answer to her cautious, 'Hello, Brian,' he said. 'Hi, Lee. I've got two free tickets to see *American Follies* on Friday night—one of the perks of working for *Travel News*. Can I pick you up at seven?' As Lee hesitated, he said anxiously, 'You'll be free, won't you? Tickets are going to be hard to come by—it's a very popular show.'

Lee knew that it was, and the note of disappointment in Brian's voice, combined with the guilty knowledge that she had been making excuses to avoid seeing him lately, made her decide to accept the invitation, maybe more enthusiastically than she had intended. 'Of course I'm free, Brian,' she said warmly. 'And thank you. I'll be looking forward to it.'

'Great. So will I.'

As she put the phone down, Adam appeared in the doorway.

'Your secretary seems to have disappeared,' he said. 'As your door was open, I assumed you were free.'

'I am. Marion is probably making tea. Would you like a cup?'

'No, thanks.' She thought he looked faintly annoyed, and wondered if she had done something to cause it. 'I just called in to let you know I'll be away for a few days. In case there was anything you wanted to discuss before I leave.'

'Thank you,' she said formally. 'But I can't think of anything. I seem to be managing quite well without you.' That sounded pointed.

'I thought,' he said deliberately, 'that you might like to get on with your new job without the boss breathing down your neck every day. I've made it a habit to give my editors a push in the right direction and then leave them to find their own way.'

'*Their* own way, or yours?'

'Let's say *I* set the direction, and they find the way.'

That was clever, she thought, but then he was.

'I suppose it's a case of why keep a dog and bark yourself,' she commented flippantly. 'You'd be much too smart for that.'

'Oh, I wouldn't call you a *dog*, Lee,' he said rather gently.

Her eyes flashed upward to his, encountering a glinting anger. He didn't need to add the obvious, but he had left her without a chance of retaliation. He could be a brute when he chose. Perhaps it came naturally to him.

'Why are you angry with me?' she asked, deciding to risk a frontal attack.

'I'm not.'

'Then why this—polite beastliness?' she demanded.

His eyebrows lifted slightly. 'Polite I acknowledge. I wasn't aware that I was being beastly—except in self-defence.'

'Surely that's to admit it! And I don't know what you mean by self-defence!'

'Don't you? I was under the impression that you started this. Were you annoyed with me for keeping away for a few days?'

Lee shrugged. 'I hardly noticed.'

'Didn't you? I could swear I detected an air of resentment about you from the minute I walked in here. I quite thought you were feeling neglected.'

'Well, think again,' she suggested, borrowing some of his own mocking intonation. 'Didn't it occur to you that I might have enjoyed my freedom these last few days, and been annoyed when you turned up here this morning?'

Adam gave a sardonic nod of acknowledgement, but she could see he didn't believe her. No wonder, for she didn't believe it herself. His guess had come much too close for comfort.

'I wasn't aware I had curtailed your freedom,' he said. 'Never mind. You can have all the freedom you want until next week. I won't be back until Monday.'

Lee tried to look pleased. 'Have a good time,' she said, and hoping that he would take the hint and go, picked up the nearest folder to her hand and opened it.

He didn't leave, but instead came round the desk and stood beside her, reading the first page with her.

'Looks interesting,' he commented. 'What is it?'

Silently she turned back to the title page and let him read it for himself.'

'*Loving sexuality for our time*,' he read aloud. 'Did you commission this?'

'Heavens, no! It came in the mail.'

'How good is it?'

'I don't know yet. I've just begun reading it—though I suppose it's a waste of time.'

'Meaning you don't expect it to be good?' he asked. 'I never suspected you of negativism.'

'Even if it is good,' she answered, 'it's hardly suitable for us, is it?'

'Why on earth not?'

'Helen said it was pretty frank—even from the first page you can see that.'

'So what?' Adam asked with some amusement. 'Do you think it's pornographic?'

'No. But it's just not our style.'

'You're supposed to be changing the style—remember?'

'Not to this extent!'

'To *any* extent—if it will sell the magazine.'

'That's the only thing that matters to you, isn't it?'

His eyes raked her with a hard gaze. 'I see. We're back to that again.'

'Back to what?'

'You know what I mean. You've made your opinion of me abundantly clear on several occasions. It happens to be my job to produce magazines that sell. And it's your job to edit them. This——' he said, picking up the manuscript and almost throwing it down again on her desk, '—looks to me like the kind of thing we need to lift *Lady* out of the doldrums and into the twentieth-century market place. Why don't we make it the lead feature of the special issue?'

'I *won't* try to sell the magazine on sex!'

'That isn't what I'm suggesting.'

'Isn't it? You're suggesting we make it the lead story, and you haven't even read beyond the title and the first page!'

'The title page gives the author—who happens to have some impressive letters after her name, in case you hadn't noticed, and the first page lists some of the sources. They also look pretty impressive to me. If the rest is as good as that, I think we should print it.'

'I don't!'

'I presume you have a reason?'

'I told you, it's not our style.'

'How do you know? You haven't read it through yet, any more than I have.'

'Well, I *will*, then,' Lee declared, exasperated.

'With an open mind? Or having already decided you won't print it?'

'I'll try to keep an open mind,' she said. 'But——'

'But——?'

'I think you're forgetting this is a women's magazine.'

'You're not telling me women are not interested in sex?'

'Not in the same way that men are,' she said.

'My dear girl, where have you been these last ten years?' Adam demanded.

'Oh, don't be silly! I know perfectly well it's a fashionable topic, but I thought the idea was for *Lady* to become more thoughtful and serious——'

'Good lord! You make it sound dead boring!'

'You know what I mean!'

'Do I take it you think sex is a frivolous subject? At least *that*'—he indicated the folder on her desk—'won't bore the readers to tears.'

'Of course I don't think it's frivolous,' Lee almost snapped. 'Just unsuitable!'

Unexpectedly, Adam laughed. 'You have no idea how Victorian you sound!' he told her.

Of course she hadn't meant 'unsuitable' in a general sense, only in the context of *Lively Lady* and this particular article. She might have laughed herself if he hadn't added, 'You mustn't judge every woman by yourself, you know, Lee.'

'What do you mean?' she asked blankly.

'Isn't it obvious? You should read that. Maybe you'd learn a thing or two. It's about time you did.'

He went out without even saying goodbye, leaving her seething with confusion and rage. What did he mean? That she was a prude? or frigid? or perhaps both. Neither was true, she knew. She told herself he was exacting petty revenge for apparent indifference on her part. But she didn't think pettiness was characteristic of Adam Broome.

CHAPTER SEVEN

LEE dressed with some care on Friday night, choosing a pale green, silky synthetic dress with a swirling skirt that was one of her favourites, and clipping earring pendants of New Zealand jade greenstone on to her ears. She had still not shaken off a feeling of vague guilt about Brian, and in some nearly subconscious region of her mind she knew that dressing up for him represented some sort of reparation.

Michael was absorbed in a pile of textbooks spread across the small table in the kitchen when the doorbell rang just before seven.

Expecting Brian, Lee was surprised to find Mark Gould standing on the step, with a briefcase in his hand.

'Wow!' he exclaimed, taking in her unusually glamorous appearance. 'That's nice! I suppose it's too much to hope it's all for me?'

Lee smiled. 'I didn't even know you were coming, I'm afraid. I take it Michael invited you over? He's in the kitchen, surrounded by books.'

She opened the door wide and stepped back to let him in.

'Who's the lucky guy?' he asked as he stepped past her. 'The one who's taking you out tonight?'

'A friend from work.' He had stopped in front of her, so that she still stood holding the door.

'Just good friends?' he asked quizzically, as though the reply might matter to him.

'That's right.'

'Good.'

Lee smiled faintly at his emphasis, anticipating his next move.

Teasingly, he reached out and flicked at one of her pendant earrings, brushing her skin with his fingers. 'I like those. Will you wear them when you come out with me?'

Lightly she asked, '*Am* I going out with you?'

'I hope so. Will you?'

'Is that an invitation?'

'It's a request. What about tomorrow night? *That*'s an invitation.'

'Very well,' said Lee. 'Where are we going?'

'What do you fancy? Dinner and dancing—a film?'

'What do *you* fancy?'

'You.'

Lee laughed, then turned her head to see Brian, who had almost reached the door without her noticing.

She introduced the two men, and watched them sizing each other up as they politely shook hands. Brian looked a little ruffled, and Mark faintly amused.

Lee went to get her bag and a light shawl, and came back to find them both still standing near the door. As Brian opened it for her, Mark asked, 'Can I call for you at seven tomorrow night, Lee?'

'Fine, thank you. Goodnight.'

He said goodnight to them both, and Brian muttered something unintelligible in return, shutting the door behind them with a decisive bang.

'Who is he?' he asked as soon as he had started his car and begun driving towards the centre of the city.

'An old friend. I've known him since we were at school together.'

'And you're making him free of your flat?'

'What does that mean?' Lee asked with the beginning of anger in her voice.

'Well, you left him there, didn't you?'

'Not alone,' she said quite gently. 'My brother is living with me at the moment. He and Mark are studying together.'

Brian glanced at her and said stiffly, 'I see. I didn't know that.'

'No, I don't suppose you did.' She didn't say, *It's none of your business*, but the implication was clearly there, and she knew that he had got the point. Brian had no claim on her, and she didn't want him to fancy that he had any right to comment on her friends or social life.

It was not a propitious start to the evening, and although she enjoyed the show, which was well presented and entertaining, there was an undercurrent of tension that she knew was felt by her escort as well as herself. She tried to compensate by being extra gay and attentive to Brian's conversation as they moved out to the carpeted foyer for a drink during the interval, and as she tipped back her head and smiled up at him, her eye was caught by Adam Broome's face in the crowd, darkly contemptuous as his cold eyes flicked from her to Brian and back again.

With a sudden chill she remembered Adam accusing her of being a tease, of flirting with him and deliberately leading him on without intending to follow through her actions. The look on his face said quite clearly that he thought she was repeating the performance for Brian.

Then the crowd surged in front of him and he disappeared from her view.

Damn him! She thought furiously. What right had he to sit in judgment on her, anyway? His own conduct left a good deal to be desired in his dealings with women. Why should she be bothered by what he evidently thought of her?

Deliberately she moved closer to Brian and hooked her hand into the crook of his arm. She had no idea if Adam could still see her, but if so she was not going to allow him the satisfaction of having influenced her actions in any way.

Brian bought a cool drink for each of them and found a relatively quiet corner where they could sip them and look around while discussion swelled and babbled on every side. There was a party of people sitting around a low table not far from them, and Lee recognised Aaron Carson among them, as Brian exclaimed, 'Hey! That's our ex-boss, isn't it?'

'Yes,' she said, trying to sound casual. 'And his daughter.' She had just seen that Lisbet was there, too, looking beautiful and more animated than she had ever seen her, in a clinging cream satin dress.

So that was who Adam was with, although she could see no sign of him now.

Then she saw him, walking towards Lisbet and her party, with his back to herself; but she would have recognised that dark-blond head with its faintly arrogant tilt anywhere. There was another man with him, and they both had drinks in their hands that they deposited on the table. Watching Adam, Lee glanced past him to the Carsons, and saw Lisbet's face light up as the two men approached.

Ever since her marriage had broken up, Lisbet had worn an air of hardly hidden sadness, but now that was completely gone. There was no trace of doubt in Lee's mind that this was a woman in love, and secure in the joy of having that love returned. No woman would look at a man with so much of her heart in her eyes if she was not quite certain of his feelings and of her own.

'Hey!' exclaimed Brian, obviously intrigued. 'Do you see that!'

'Yes,' Lee said, around a peculiar lump in her throat. She wanted to run away somewhere, but there was a hurtful fascination about watching the little scene in front of them. Someone walked across her vision, and someone else obscured her view of Mr Carson and the unknown man who was now sitting across from him, left of Lisbet. She saw Adam turn his head to speak to the girl who was sitting on his right and was shocked at her own heart-churning reaction to the sight of his smiling profile.

She had always liked Lisbet Carson, and should have been glad to see her finding some happiness after heartbreak. Instead she felt thoroughly miserable. She finally had to admit that she was in love with Adam Broome, herself.

She became aware that Brian was digging his fingers into her arm, his face alight with excitement. He had been talking to her and she hadn't heard a word.

'What?' she said vaguely, but he didn't even notice.

'Do you think there'll be an announcement by the happy couple?' he was saying. 'Or maybe just a quiet register office ceremony somewhere. After the big wedding the first time, with all the attendant ballyhoo, I guess a repeat performance could look a bit ridiculous—that divorce *was* final —legally, I mean, wasn't it?'

'I don't know, I think so,' Lee answered somewhat distractedly, trying to drag her eyes away from the scene across the room, but finding that her gaze kept returning to it.

'Oh, well—good luck to them,' said Brian, raising his glass and draining the last of its contents. 'It's nice to see a happy ending.'

'Yes, isn't it?' Lee tried to smile. 'I think she deserves it.'

'What about him?' Brian asked humorously.

Lee shrugged. 'I don't particularly care about him,' she lied. 'But Lisbet is a nice girl, and I'm glad for her.'

That wasn't strictly true, either, but it would be mean-spirited of her not to try, at least, to be glad for Lisbet. None of what Lee was feeling was *her* fault, that was sure.

A buzzer heralded the beginning of the second half, and the Carsons' party began to stand up, and move away from their chairs. Lisbet was animatedly talking, reaching out her hands to Adam, who took them in his, and saying something laughingly to the man beside him, then reaching up and kissing Adam lightly on the cheek. Lee saw Lisbet's father put his arm about her shoulders and say something which caused more laughter, the whole party seeming to join in. They were all in high spirits and enjoying themselves.

It certainly looked as though they were celebrating something.

'Hey! Finish your drink,' Brian admonished her. 'We don't want to have to grope our way in the dark.'

Automatically Lee did finish her drink, and although the lights were still up as they returned to their seats, she felt as though she was groping her way through a fog of darkness and despair.

Although on one level she wanted nothing less than to go out again on Saturday evening, with the rational part of her mind she knew that it was as well she had a date with Mark that night.

Sitting at home brooding would not have done her any good, and somehow she was going to have to gather enough courage to face Adam with a well-controlled air of non-chalance on Monday.

Adding to her depression was the knowledge that Brian had been hinting last night at a deeper relationship between them, and she, too wrapped in the shock of discovering the depth of her feelings for Adam, had failed to make it clear that such a relationship was out of the question from her point of view. She had managed to dodge more than a perfunctory goodnight kiss by murmuring about a hard day at work and feeling tired. It was cowardly and unfair to put it off, and if Brian insisted on wanting more than friend-ship, she would have to be frank with him some time. But last night she had felt unable to face any unpleasantness.

Remembering Mark's teasing request, she wore the greenstone earrings again, teaming them with a green silk-knit top and the skirt she had worn the night Adam took her out to dinner. She hesitated over that, but her wardrobe was less than extensive, and she didn't want to wear the same dress Mark had briefly seen her in last night.

'I'm glad you wore them,' he told her as she let him into the flat. She moved away before he could repeat his action of the previous evening, but he didn't seem to mind.

Michael greeted his friend with pleasure, and Lee left them together while she fetched her shawl. She smiled at her brother affectionately as he waved them goodbye, stop-ping to ask from the doorway, 'You'll be all right, Michael?'

'Of course I will, idiot!' The impatience in his muffled voice was tempered by affection.

'I shouldn't do that,' she said ruefully as Mark opened the door of his car for her.

'Shouldn't do what?' he asked as he got into his own seat.

'Fuss over Michael. He hates it.'

'Yes, I've noticed. A very independent young cuss, your brother.'

'You're being very good to him.'

After a moment's silence, he said, 'Has it occurred to you that I might have an ulterior motive?'

Michael had suggested that himself, once, she remembered.

'I don't believe it,' she told him.

Mark looked sideways at her before returning his attention to the road ahead. 'Don't mistake me for a do-gooder, will you? I happen to like your brother—I also happen to think I might like you a whole lot more.'

Not quite knowing how to answer that, she didn't try, but turned her attention instead to looking out of the window. 'Where are we going?' she asked, seeing that they were travelling towards the harbour, where the orange lights were just winking on the span of the arched bridge that crossed its darkened waters.

'A new place I found last week,' he told her, as the car began travelling along the waterfront, passing the forest of masts outside the yacht club. 'You'll like it.'

It was small and cosy, the dance floor minute and the food very good. Mark was a good dancer and a pleasant companion, and ordinarily Lee would have enjoyed herself.

Near midnight, as they moved around the tiny dance floor, his hands light and firm on her waist, he bent his head to look at her searchingly, asking, 'What's the matter, Lee?'

'Nothing. What makes you say that?'

'Just the fact that you've been hardly with me all evening.'

She had hoped that she had hidden her abstraction better than that. She liked Mark and she had tried very hard to push the memory of last night and before that from her mind, but the food and wine and dancing kept reminding her of the night Adam had wined and dined her—and then taken her home and kissed her into a state of mindless delight, and asked her out to a lunch that had never taken place.

She gave Mark a slightly brittle smile. 'Whatever are you talking about? I'm right here—I have been all along.'

'Uh-uh.' He shook his head. 'Every so often your mind goes floating off into nowhere—or—somewhere—out of my reach. It may sound conceited, but when I hold a girl like this, she doesn't usually give me the impression that she's thinking of something or someone—else.'

Slightly shaken by that sort of perception, Lee tried to smile. 'I'm sorry, Mark. I did have a late night last night. I suppose I'm tired.'

He shook his head as though he didn't believe that excuse. 'Are you wishing you were with Brian what's-his-name?' he asked wryly.

That was so far from the truth that she laughed a little. 'No!'

Mark grinned in return. 'Poor guy,' he said. 'I didn't think you were as keen on him as he obviously was on you. He would have liked to push my face in, wouldn't he?'

'He didn't say. I'm sure you're exaggerating.'

'He didn't need to say. And I'm not exaggerating—at least not much. Your Brian didn't like me—not that I blame him.'

'He's not mine.'

'And you're not his; I'm glad. Is there anyone else?'

Lee shook her head firmly. She certainly wasn't Adam Broome's, and he had Lisbet now, with the full and enthusiastic approval of her family, if last night was anything to go by. It seemed obvious that that was no casual affair. Brian was probably right in expecting a wedding in the near future.

The music wound up with a flourish, and Mark asked, 'Ready to go home, now?'

'Yes, thank you,' she said, trying not to sound too eager. What with the effort of trying to concentrate only on him, and the way he was skimming uncomfortably close to guessing at the cause of her preoccupation, she was relieved at the suggestion.

The flat was in darkness when they reached it, and he left her at the door, brushing her lips very lightly with his as he said goodnight. 'Can I take you out again?' he asked, his finger playing gently with her earring, setting it swinging.

'Yes, of course,' she answered, because he was nice and it was obviously futile to stay at home wishing things were different. His touch didn't electrify her, but he was far from repulsive, and in time she might find him just as attractive as Adam—she hoped.

'Thanks.' He pushed open the door behind her and turned her to the darkness of the flat. As Lee closed the door she heard him whistling on his way back to the car.

Monday was worse than she had expected. There was trouble with the printers and the beauty editor reported sick, throwing an extra burden of work on Lee and Helen. A vital photograph was mislaid and finally found behind a filing cabinet after frantic searching, and no amount of cutting and arranging seemed to suffice to make the following week's layout look satisfactory to Lee's critical eye.

When Adam walked into her office after lunch she all but glared at him, asking ungraciously, 'What do you want?'

He looked slightly amused. 'Your dulcet greetings are a continual joy to me, Lee,' he drawled.

Reluctantly, she smiled an apology. 'I'm sorry. It's one of those days, I'm afraid,' she admitted. 'I've been fiddling with this layout for hours and nothing seems to work.'

'Let me see. Perhaps a fresh eye might do the trick.'

Lee leaned back, pushing the page towards him, and handing him her pencil and ruler.

He studied it in silence for a few minutes, and she thought, not without a faint satisfaction, that Adam, too, was stumped.

Finally he said, 'If you move this photograph to the right, and perhaps crop it a bit—would that help? Then this paragraph could come down into that space—right?'

She leaned forward. He was right, and her relief was mingled with some chagrin that she hadn't seen that for herself.

'Thank you,' she said. 'I'll do that.'

He straightened up, his hands in his pockets, watching her, and as she looked up there was a sudden ache in the back of her throat as she remembered Lisbet putting her hands in his, and the way his strong fingers had closed about the girl's.

For a moment there seemed to be an answering warmth in his gaze, and unexpectedly he leaned forward and smoothed his hand over her hair, brushing a strand from her eyes. 'I can see it's one of those days,' he said. 'You're looking quite dishevelled.'

Involuntarily, she jerked away from his hand, and his eyes narrowed with annoyance.

'I don't have leprosy,' he said coldly.

'You don't have the right to touch me, either,' she retorted, before she could stop herself.

'I can recall one or two occasions when you haven't minded at all,' he drawled. A sudden, speculative look came into his eyes, and Lee said in panic, 'Well, I mind now. Kindly keep your hands to yourself!'

It was a stupid thing to say to a man who had never passed up a challenge in his life. She realised that even as he moved in a quick, fluid lunge, and grasping her wrist, pulled her from her chair.

She raised her other hand, but he expected that, and she found herself imprisoned against his hard body, with both hands held behind her.

'I haven't even *begun* to touch you yet,' he told her.

He transferred both her wrists to one hand, holding them quite easily in spite of her struggles, and began a slow caress of her back with the other.

Clenching her teeth, she muttered, '*Stop it!*'

Adam took no notice, only bending his head to hers, and she jerked her face aside to prevent his mouth reaching its objective.

He ran his lips down the side of her neck and then to the base of her throat, instead, and in spite of herself, their searing sweetness made her shudder faintly with a mixture of pleasure and trepidation.

The hand on her back moved under her hair and grasped her head, forcing it round so that her lips met his waiting mouth, and her whispered, protesting 'No!' was breathed into it. His lips moved on hers, caressing, sure and demanding of her co-operation—surrender.

She refused to give it, for her pride's sake, even while her body clamoured to give in and accept whatever might be offered it. These kisses, this dangerous physical delight, were not hers to enjoy, or his to bestow. He was being unfair to both her and Lisbet, and as long as she remembered that, she could ignore her own wild longing.

At last he raised his head, releasing her very slowly. His eyes had regained their coldness, but his breathing was a little uneven, and she took some futile pleasure in that, even while she despised herself for being glad that she could stir his senses, that he did desire her even though he was planning to marry someone else. Even as she reminded herself that he was not the first man to want to have his cake and eat it.

When she could trust her voice she said icily, 'That was despicable!'

'I daresay you're right,' he shrugged. 'But worth it. You're a hard girl to understand, Lee.'

'Then don't try!' she snapped.

'Are you frightened—of understanding?'

'I'm just disgusted with your way of going about it.'

A slight frown creased his forehead. 'Disgusted? Do kisses disgust you?'

'Yours do!'

His eyes searched her face. 'Why?'

'Never mind,' she snapped, trying to move back behind her desk, but he gripped her arm and repeated, 'Why?'

'Because they mean nothing.'

He released her, and said, 'Is that what you think?'

'That's what I know!' Suddenly frightened of self-betrayal, she added, 'They mean nothing to you, and even less to me. It isn't only men who can feel a—a passing physical desire.'

'I see.' He paused, looking her over slowly. 'And I take it you've lost any *passing desire* you might once have had for me?'

With an effort, Lee shrugged. 'I'm afraid so.'

His mouth twisted. 'You haven't profited from the

article we discussed. I thought it might teach you a thing or two. It's time you learned something about men, and loving. Of course,' he added, 'experience might be a better teacher.'

'I'm sure there's nothing like it,' she said. 'But some kinds of experience I can do without.'

CHAPTER EIGHT

HER confrontation with Adam didn't improve the day for Lee, and when Brian rang later while she was having a conference with Helen and the fashion editor, she was noticeably short with him.

He waylaid her as she was leaving her office after work, and her heart sank as she saw the fairly belligerent look on his face.

Casually, she said, 'Hello, Brian.'

'Hello.' He didn't smile, but as she kept walking towards the lift he had no choice but to fall into step beside her.

'You didn't sound very pleased when I phoned,' he said, as they entered the lift together.

'I'm sorry,' Lee said crisply. 'I was rather busy.'

'Are you going to be busy tonight?'

'I'm having an early night.'

'I see. Did you enjoy yourself on Saturday?'

'Yes, thank you.'

As the doors slid open to let them out on the ground floor, he asked, 'Where did he take you?'

'We went dancing.' The glance she swung at him was cool and wary.

'Are you seeing *him* again tonight?'

'I just told you, I'm having an early night. And if I *was* seeing Mark, it wouldn't be any of your business, Brian. This conversation is beginning to sound remarkably like a cross-examination, and I don't like it.'

'Don't you?' He leaned close to her and she caught a

whiff of whisky on his breath. 'Do you like *me*, Lee?'

'At the moment, not very much,' she said crossly, thoroughly fed up.

'That's what I thought,' he said, with a touch of pathos. 'You prefer Mark, don't you?'

'It isn't a question of preferring anyone,' she shrugged. 'You don't have any rights over me, Brian, and neither does Mark. I've only been out with him once.'

'Huh! It won't be the last time, though, will it?'

'As a matter of fact, probably not.'

'Probably not!' he echoed. His voice was quite clear, but there was a glazed look in his eyes that made her wonder how much he had been drinking.

'We've been good friends, Brian,' she said reasonably. 'Let's not spoil that.'

He laughed nastily. 'Oh, sure! Let's be just good friends. Once you were a mite more friendly, Lee.'

'Only once,' she said coldly. 'And it was obviously a mistake. I'm sorry if you misconstrued it, Brian. You can be quite certain it won't happen again.'

'Won't it? Well, now we know, don't we? Off with the old and on with the new, is it?'

'Don't be silly!' She was thankful that the foyer was almost deserted, and the one or two people leaving the building did not seem curious about the tense conversation going on in the doorway. 'Why don't you go home and get yourself some strong coffee?' she suggested.

Bitterly, Brian said, 'Oh, sure! That'll fix everything.' Turning away from her, he flung over his shoulder, 'Good luck to you with Markie-boy—he looks the sort who could dish up some of your own medicine.'

Lee stood there for a few minutes after he had gone, trying to stay calm and telling herself it was for the best. She was sorry to have friendship end with such bitterness, but the situation was impossible if Brian was going to show such ridiculous and unreasonable jealousy. It was as well to have it over with.

But it wasn't quite over. The following week an engagement was announced between *Lady's* beauty editor and the editor of *Travel News*. The staffs of both magazines got together to throw an after-work party for them, in the *Travel News* office.

Lee took the time to tidy up and renew her make-up before going to the party, because she had arranged to meet Mark and see a film with him later in the evening.

When she entered the *Travel News* office it was crowded and noisy, and she paused in the doorway, looking about her.

The newly engaged couple were surrounded by well-wishers, and as she moved towards them Lee saw that Adam was among them. For a moment she hesitated, and he glanced up and caught her eye.

Lee, chiding herself, moved up to the group, looking away from him and smiling at the others as she offered her congratulations. Very conscious of Adam standing only inches from her, she accepted a glass of wine that someone thrust into her hand, and joined in a toast.

As soon as she could, she edged herself away, and found that she had backed herself up against a desk. The next moment an arm slid around her waist, and Brian said, 'Hi, sweetie. Long time no see.'

He always had a tendency to talk in clichés, she remembered, suddenly realising that she found it an intensely irritating habit. But he seemed to have at least got over his jealous huff, so she smiled at him with slight restraint and returned his greeting.

'You look nice,' he commented. 'Got a date?'

'I am going out later,' she said, cautiously.

'With Mark again?'

As she hesitated he said, 'Don't worry, I'm not going to make a scene. Sorry about the other night. Had too much to drink over a business lunch, I guess—and a couple more besides before I tackled you. I overreacted a bit, I'm afraid.'

'You did, rather.' She touched his arm gently. 'It's all right. Brian. The fault was partly mine, anyway.'

'Hey, you two!' someone interrupted gaily, and Lee looked up to see one of Brian's colleagues, holding a brimming glass of beer and beaming at them. She knew him slightly as an extrovert with a loud voice that he was using to good effect now. 'When are *you* going to name the day?' he asked, as she inwardly flinched. Several people, Adam among them, had turned at the sound of the hearty voice.

Brian's arm was still about her waist, and she felt paralysed.

He answered for them, saying lightly, 'Hold it, mate. Lee's thrown me over for an old flame from way back in her schooldays. I'm no longer in the running. We're just friends.'

She saw Adam turn abruptly away, and hardly heard the bantering reply to Brian's casual announcement. Afterwards she thought he had handled it rather well, but she couldn't help wishing he had done it differently, and in spite of his apparently good grace perhaps he had been taking a small revenge. Of course everyone must have known that they saw each other quite often, and she couldn't really blame him for looking to his own pride when he was put on a spot in front of all his workmates.

The special issue of the magazine was well on in its preparation and the staff were becoming enthusiastic about its new look, excitement mounting as the publication date approached. At Adam's suggestion—very nearly a command—Lee was working on a full-page editorial setting out a brief history of the magazine and defining its future direction. Usually the editorial occupied a very small space of a few paragraphs' length at the front of the issue, but now he wanted her to take a full page each week. 'You have talent,' he told her. 'I want it put to good use—for us.'

Helen, who was present, added her urging. Helen had also been enthusiastic about the inclusion of the article on loving sexuality when she discovered that Adam approved. Lee could have vetoed the idea, but she believed in teamwork and knew that in this case her judgment was affected by the quarrel she had had with Adam over the piece. Everyone else seemed to think it was a good idea, and she had to admit that the article, while controversial, and very different from anything they had tried before, was well researched, well written, and far from indecent, in a legal or moral sense.

Advertisements had already begun appearing in the papers and on the radio and television. Then Lee learned one morning that a television appearance had been arranged for her, in a chat show.

'No!' she exclaimed when Adam broke the news.

'What on earth do you mean, *no*?'

'She's just nervous,' Helen said soothingly. 'She'll be all right once she gets used to the idea.'

'I don't want to go on television!' Lee said forcefully.

'Why ever not?' Helen asked. 'I'd jump at the chance!'

'Well, you can have it! I'm not doing it,' Lee insisted, turning to Adam.

Exasperated, he said, 'Yes, you are. It's part of your job. It's all arranged for Saturday evening.'

'Live?' she squeaked.

'Yes—what's the difference, anyway?'

'The difference is if I make a fool of myself it can't be cut out, if it's been shown live and not filmed.'

'You won't make a fool of yourself,' Helen assured her.

'No, you're doing that now,' Adam told her.

'Thanks a lot!'

'Well, stop being so silly. You knew this was part of the plan.'

'I did not!'

'We discussed this when we first talked about *Lady's* new look.'

'You mean *you* discussed it with the advertising man. I distinctly remember that I didn't want to be promoted or whatever your revolting term was!'

Helen blinked at her vehemence and Adam's lips compressed.

'It isn't *my* term,' he said. 'As *I* remember, you promised me your full co-operation.'

'I happen to be busy on Saturday night. You didn't say anything about working weekends.'

'Cancel it,' he said. 'Your boy-friend can come and sit in the audience—I'll see he gets a free ticket.' Forestalling her as she took a breath to continue the argument, Adam added, 'You'll be there, Lee. Or we'll find another editor for the magazine.'

Helen gave a faint gasp, and Lee said coldly, 'That isn't necessary.'

'Good. I'll pick you up before the show in case you chicken out at the last minute. I'll be there to hold your hand anyway. I'm supposed to go on camera with you. By the way, wear something glamorous.'

After he had gone, Helen said, 'He didn't mean it, you know, about finding another editor.'

'Oh, didn't he?' Lee asked sceptically.

'Of course not. He was scared you were going to flatly refuse the show, that's all.'

'Scared?' Lee raised an eyebrow.

Helen laughed. 'Well—slightly nervous, then. I can't imagine him being really frightened by anything.'

'Neither can I. Or if he was, he certainly wouldn't show it. *I'll* probably be a total nervous wreck by Saturday. How did I get myself *into* this?'

'You didn't,' Helen grinned. '*He* did.'

He sent down a ticket which she found on her desk one morning and tore up. She absolutely refused to have either Michael or Mark in the audience, sure that their presence would only make her more nervous. She supposed that Mark could loosely be termed a 'boy-friend' as she had been seeing a lot of him lately, not only when he took her out, but when he came to the flat on Michael's invitation. He had kissed her a few times, pleasantly and without any great passion, and she took care not to give the impression she expected or wanted anything more. She wanted no repetition of her experience with Brian.

The television set in the flat was an old black and white model, and Mark offered to let Michael watch the show on his colour set, and put him up for the night. Michael accepted with alacrity.

Lee debated buying something new to wear and decided against it. She wasn't sure what Adam had meant exactly by 'something glamorous' and perversely she had made up her mind not to try to outdo the very beautiful and sophisticated hostess of the show, whose up-to-date and sometimes daring gowns were one of its main features.

She took out the green synthetic after Michael had left with Mark on Saturday evening and dropped it across her bed, only to find that there was a dark stain on the skirt. She didn't remember spilling anything on it, but there it was, an unidentifiable mark, and far too late to do anything about removing it now, even if she had known what it was.

Fighting down a sudden panic, she riffled through her wardrobe and took out a navy blue silk shirtwaister with a wide white collar in crisp organdie, with a small pink artificial rose at the neckline. It was the sort of undatable dress she preferred to buy, and though it wasn't as pretty as the green, it was a go-anywhere kind of thing and should be suitable.

She had a shower and was putting on her make-up, sitting at her dressing table in a white towelling robe, when the doorbell rang.

Lipstick poised, she checked her watch, thinking it couldn't possibly be Adam. But when she opened the door to his second ring, it was.

'You're early!' she exclaimed accusingly, and then had to turn away as she let him in, leaving him to shut the door himself, because the telephone was ringing.

In answer to her breathless 'Hello,' Mark's voice said, 'We thought we'd just wish you luck again before you go.'

'Oh, Mark! That's sweet of you.'

'Still nervous?'

'Not so much now, thanks.' She had been, in spite of the staff's assurances that she would breeze through the whole thing, in spite of Michael's confident pride in her, and Mark's teasing reassurances.

But now Adam was here, leaning on the wall and watching her, and the whole thing would be over in a couple of hours. He didn't look a bit nervous, and after all, he was facing the cameras too.

Mark was saying, 'Good, that's the spirit. We're looking forward to seeing you. Here's Michael.'

Michael hated telephones, because it was often difficult for the person on the other end to understand him, and Lee appreciated the effort that he made to speak to her, adding his good wishes to Mark's.

'Thank you, darling,' she said warmly, trying to put that appreciation into her voice. 'I hope you enjoy the show.'

When she put the phone down and turned to Adam, he asked, 'Is he coming to watch?'

Lee shook her head. 'I don't want anyone who's close to me there. I'd be more nervous than ever.'

'Is it bad? I came early in case you were thinking of running out on it.'

'I wouldn't do that. The whole staff of *Lady* will be watching tonight. I couldn't let them down.'

'Good. That's very fetching,' he commented, flicking a glance over the short robe and the long legs beneath it. 'But shouldn't you be changing?'

'Yes,' she said, hesitating because although he was being perfectly polite and rather urbane, she had an odd feeling something was wrong. Adam was holding himself too still, his face too expressionless.

Wondering, she asked, 'Are *you* nervous?'

'Not particularly.'

He was evidently not going to add to that, so she gestured vaguely to the chairs saying, 'I won't be long. Make yourself at home.'

He didn't, though. And when Lee came out of the bedroom he was standing in the centre of the room, looking as though he had spent the time prowling round it instead of relaxing in a comfortable chair.

She had put on a pearl necklace at the last minute, not sure if it was necessary or added anything to the effect of the dress, but suddenly it seemed inadequate by itself, and she didn't have much she could dress it up with.

She had her hand up, playing with the pearls, as she emerged into the lounge, leaving the door of the bedroom open behind her.

Adam looked at her assessingly, and said, 'No, take it off.'

'Oh.' She was surprised, but she hadn't been too sure about the pearls, and she unclasped them and put them on a side table. 'Better?'

'Only slightly,' he said drily. 'The pearls are terrible. But I meant the dress. Take it off.'

'*What?*'

'You heard me. I told you to wear something glamorous. You look like a schoolgirl going out for an evening with Daddy, not the editor of a magazine for with-it young women.'

'I really don't think it matters what the editor *looks* like!' she objected, annoyed at his description of her appearance.

'Of course it does!' he said impatiently. 'The whole idea is for you to reflect the new image of the magazine. That's why we got you on this show.'

'Well, I'm sorry,' she said, her eyes flashing danger signals while she tried to keep her voice cool, 'but I have no intention of being some sort of sex symbol to sell the magazine. If you want that you'll have to employ a model.'

She made to walk past him to go to the door, but he caught her firmly by the arm, turning her back the way she came.

'Go and change, Lee,' he said quietly, but the light in his eye meant business, she could see.

She twisted out of his grasp and turned to face him defiantly.

'I won't—and you can't make me!'

'Are you so sure of that?' Icy cold blue eyes held hers, and for a moment she wavered. But she had never taken kindly to intimidation, and to give in to him would hurt her pride too much. Somehow Adam had taken her heart; he wasn't going to have her pride as well. Again she tried to pass him, expecting opposition and braced for it, ready.

Unexpectedly, he let her walk past him, and she relaxed a little, thinking he had realised he couldn't force her to change. But she had not allowed for utter ruthlessness on his part. Instead of trying to grab her arms and turn her again, he had stepped behind her, and before she knew what he was planning he had a firm grip on the collar of her dress and had ripped it down off her shoulders, tearing off the buttons and ruining it completely, exposing the white lace bra underneath.

Lee gave a gasp of pure shock, and turning, swung her hand up and slapped him as hard as she could, not even pausing to pull up the ruins of her dress first and cover herself.

Even as the flush of blood rose on his face where her hand had made contact with his skin, he was insolently inspecting what he had revealed, and she hastily pulled the edges of the bodice together to hide it, ignoring his cynical smile at her action.

He raised a hand and touched his cheek briefly. '*That*'s a score we'll settle later,' he said quite pleasantly. 'Right now, let's find you something else to wear. There isn't much time.'

'You must be mad!' she spat at him. 'If you think I'm still going to appear on your beastly show—after *this*!'

For answer he grabbed her wrist and pulled her, resisting, into the bedroom. 'What's wrong with that?' he asked, catching sight of the green dress she had left on the bed.

'It's stained,' she informed him with satisfaction.

He dropped her wrist and picked it up, inspecting the skirt to confirm it.

'You see?' she said tauntingly, as he let it fall on to the bed again.

'You must have something else,' he said. 'What about that outfit you wore the night I took you out to dinner?' Without waiting for her answer he opened her wardrobe and began pushing the hanging clothes aside.

'You're wasting your time,' she told him. 'I'm not going. You might be able to carry me kicking and screaming to the studio, but you can't stop me creating a fuss when we get there and telling the world how you got me there—on camera, if necessary.'

He found the black, rose-strewn skirt and the filmy silvery top he was looking for and put them down on the bed. Then he turned to her and said, 'I'm not asking you to do it for me. Are you going to let down the entire staff of *Lady*, as well as the hosts of the show, and the public who are expecting you to appear tonight—and don't you have a family eagerly watching for your appearance tonight, not to mention the boy-friend?'

It was emotional blackmail, and she hated him for it. He couldn't have been in any doubt that it was hatred that blazed in her eyes for him. She stood there looking at him and saying nothing, defeated but unwilling to admit it.

Adam picked up the blouse and skirt and put them in her hands.

'Put them on,' he ordered.

'Not with you here!'

Adam laughed softly. 'I won't be seeing anything I haven't seen already.'

Lee took a deep, angry breath. 'If I'm going to wear this blouse, I have to change my bra. I'm not doing it in front of you!'

For a moment he looked as though he might be going to challenge that, too, and her heart seemed to lunge suddenly. Then he said, cuttingly, 'You're in no danger. At the moment I feel more like strangling you than making love to you. You put that damned dress on purposely to annoy me, didn't you?'

'You're ridiculous!' she snapped. 'I wouldn't bother to go out of my way to annoy you *or* please you! Are you going to get out of my room while I change? Because if you don't, I promise you I'll tear this blouse to pieces myself, and then I'll really have nothing I can wear to your precious interview.'

Unexpectedly Adam's mouth twitched with a semblance of real humour. 'I'll go,' he said, moving away unhurriedly. 'But don't get any clever notions like climbing out the window, will you? I'll be back in here in five minutes and it wouldn't take long to catch you up.'

'I won't run away,' she said, casting him an icy look.

He pulled the door to but didn't latch it behind him, as though not quite trusting her, and Lee threw the clothes down on the bed again, rummaging frantically in her drawer for the light, low-cut bra, praying she could be dressed in five minutes. Because she had no doubt that Adam would do exactly as he had said. He was probably counting off the seconds now.

When he tapped on the door she called, 'I'm coming!'

and she was tidying up her hair, seeing without really noticing as she looked in the mirror that her cheeks were flushed and her eyes very bright.

He waited for her outside the bedroom door and when she appeared he said nothing. If he had she would have flown at him, she thought, just about at the end of her tether. She stayed in a temper all the way to the studio and was still simmering when she appeared on camera, so that she had no room for nervousness, and the interview went well. Afterwards she didn't remember what she had said, only that just before they went on Adam gripped her arm briefly and fiercely and muttered, 'Don't take your temper out on me in front of the cameras, Lee. Save it for later.'

They sat side by side and whenever she caught his eye she flashed him a brilliant smile so that the viewers would think them the best of friends.

Everyone was apparently quite satisfied afterwards, and Adam looked pleased with himself, too, as he drove her home.

'You did well, Lee,' he said once. 'Thank you.'

'Don't thank me,' she shrugged. 'It wasn't for you.'

'I know.'

He didn't speak again until he drew up outside her flat and she opened the door almost before he put the brake on.

She was quick, but not quick enough, and before she reached the door of the flat he was right beside her.

'I'm coming in,' he said.

'I haven't invited you,' she reminded him bitingly.

'I'm not waiting for an invitation.' As she stopped at the door, her key in her hand, he said, 'There's a small matter of a score to be settled. I don't take kindly to being slapped.' He took the key and got the door open and pushed her inside as she was saying indignantly, 'You started it! Ripping my dress——'

'I'll buy you a new one,' he promised, closing the door decisively behind them. 'Don't panic,' he added with mockery as she instinctively backed into the room, away from him. 'I'm not going to rape you.'

Lee stopped moving then, because she wasn't going to appear frightened of him.

She looked up at him and saw in his eyes what he intended as his gaze passed slowly over her, lingering on the faint shadow between her breasts that the low-necked blouse revealed, and on her lips, parted slightly as her breath quickened under his scrutiny.

She knew Adam wouldn't descend to rape, and the knowledge should have made her feel safer, but it didn't. Tiny thrills of sensual excitement chased each other up her spine, and she was deathly afraid that if he kissed her she would ignite like a torch.

'Don't touch me!' she snapped. 'Don't you dare!'

He didn't move, only stood there, but she had the impression every muscle had just gathered itself, ready to spring.

'Are you going to fight me?' he enquired lazily.

Defiantly she flashed at him, 'What do you think?'

Something that was almost a smile touched his mouth. 'I think I'd win,' he said confidently.

He would too, she knew with bitterness. 'You'd like that, wouldn't you?' she said accusingly. 'The all-conquering male, forcing a woman into submission.'

'I'd like it better if the woman would—reciprocate.'

'Not a hope!' she told him scornfully.

'None?' he asked mockingly.

Their eyes locked, hers angrily defiant, his with cool

insolence, sparked with unhidden desire.

Unwanted, answering desire stirred within her, and she took a deep breath, trying to hide it. 'I won't reciprocate,' she said. 'But I won't fight you either. It would only prolong the unpleasantness, wouldn't it?'

The smile was definite this time, but derisive, as though he didn't believe for a minute that she would find it unpleasant to be kissed by him, and that was so arrogant that it stiffened her resolve considerably.

Then he moved, saying, 'Come on, Lee. Take your medicine like a good girl.' And he reached for her and pulled her into his arms.

He wasn't angry now, she knew that. He was enjoying this. But still she wasn't prepared for the gentle way he touched her mouth with his, at first barely skimming the soft surface of her lips, then firmly parting them with a tender insistence.

She clenched her hands at her sides, but that allowed him to press her closely to his body, running one hand gently down her back while the other encircled her waist and moved to her hip, strong fingers caressing her softness, pulling her against him so that she felt scorched and enveloped in the male hardness of his body and his encircling arms.

She moved, pressing her hands against his arms, and trying to free her mouth from his.

She heard him make a deep, growling sound in his throat that might have been a *no* and one hand shifted until it encircled her neck and then supported her head, preventing any escape from him. The mouth moving over hers hardened as he deliberately deepened the kiss, overriding her resistance until she was only conscious of the demands his mouth was making on her, the intoxicating male scent of his skin, the delicious arousal of her flesh under his hands. She had no idea if she responded or not, for her whole world was afire and he was the centre of it.

When at last his grip slackened and his mouth began to draw away Lee regained some semblance of sanity and, frantic to be free of him, dug her nails into his arms where her hands still rested.

Adam must have barely noticed through the cloth of his jacket, but he held her away from him a little and looked at her with eyes that glittered with male challenge.

With an effort she withstood his gaze, glaring back at him with nothing, she hoped, but antagonism and contempt in hers. She tried to breathe evenly as he studied her face, her dishevelled hair, her tingling, parted mouth. His gaze slipped lower, then he bent his head and deliberately brushed his lips over the curves of soft skin exposed by the crossover top.

Lee went rigid, biting her lip to stop herself from curving her body closer, offering him more than he had already taken.

Still holding her in his arms, Adam raised his head and studied her face again.

'Full marks for self-control, Miss Palmer,' he said softly.

She swallowed and with desperate courage replied evenly, 'You just can't believe that you simply leave me cold, can you?'

His eyes flickered over her face again. Then he moved his right hand, sliding it softly from her waist to rest over her heart. It paused there, then cupped under the soft curve of her breast, and even as she gasped and tried to shiver away from him, his other arm imprisoned her there and his caressing thumb moved deliberately across her breast, finding the tiny, unmistakable betrayal of her body that the flimsy blouse and the wisp of bra beneath could not hide.

As her cheeks burned with humiliation, he said softly, 'This doesn't lie. Maybe it isn't love, but you feel *something* for me.'

It was impossible to answer that. He released her and she stood waiting for him to go, utterly drained.

He left without another word, and Lee dragged herself to bed, hoping devoutly that she might sleep for a week.

CHAPTER NINE

WHEN Lee opened her eyes in the morning her first instinct was to shudder and close them again.

Normally a tidy person, she had been too shattered last night to do more than remove the green dress and the torn navy-blue one from her bed to the dressing-table stool. As she reluctantly sat up and surveyed her room, she decided that it could hardly look worse if it had been hit by a tornado. The green dress had slipped to the floor and her discarded bra dangled from the stool. In her angry haste she had slammed shut her drawer and a corner of lace-edged slip had jammed in it. Her wardrobe was still wide open and she could see her clothes which had been thrust to one side in Adam's furious search. She could also see a masculine dressing gown—Michael's—on the floor of the wardrobe, and a pair of his shoes resting beside it. Thoughtfully Lee wondered what on earth Adam would have made of *that* if he had noticed. It was probably fortunate that he had been apparently too infuriated to do so.

Sighing, Lee got out of bed and began to repair the havoc.

The torn dress was beyond repair and she rolled it up and thrust it deep into a drawer. She would find a way to dispose of it some time. She put away the other things and tried, as she closed the wardrobe door, to close her mind just as decisively on the events of last night. Waves of heat washed over her as she recalled Adam's cruelly skilfull awakening of her senses, and his final triumphant taunt.

It wasn't fair for him to do this to her when he was committed to Lisbet Carson, of which there seemed little doubt. And she couldn't understand how she herself could still care for him, in spite of his behaviour. But she did. Idiotically, she longed for Monday, even while she dreaded their next encounter.

With her room restored to its usual neat appearance, she emerged into the lounge to see her pink satin rose lying in the middle of the carpet. It looked flat and sad, and had evidently been trodden on. Picking it up, she thought wryly that there must be something symbolic in that, and dropped the poor bedraggled thing into the wastebasket.

It was probably as well that she had arranged to pick up Michael from Mark's flat and drive down to their mother's for the day. It certainly wouldn't do her any good to spend the day mooning around here.

Her television debut seemed to have been a hit, at least with those who knew her. There were congratulations on all sides when she walked into the office on Monday, and the general opinion appeared to be that she had done them proud.

Of course, her mother had been ecstatic, and Michael and Mark nicely appreciative too. But it would have suited Lee if everyone would just be quiet and forget the whole thing. It was what she wanted to do rather desperately.

When a large box arrived for her after lunch she had an inkling of what it contained even before she took off the wrapping and lifted the lid.

It was a beautiful dress; she could see that even as it lay folded in the box, all softly shimmering, a golden-brown dream of a dress. She couldn't resist half-lifting it to see the style, a pretty, softly gathered bodice with shoe-string straps to go over the shoulders.

Tight-lipped, she dropped it back into the box and re-placed the lid. She re-tied the string and then carried it up to Adam's office.

'Don't disturb him,' she said to his secretary as she reached for the intercom. 'Just give him this when he's free, would you?'

Hiding her curiosity, the secretary asked, 'Is he expecting it?'

'Oh, I think so,' Lee smiled, sardonically. 'He'll know who sent it, anyway.'

As she had done. As, doubtless, he had known she would. He had probably known, too, that she would not accept it. So was it meant as a peace-offering, or a provocation, or maybe even a bribe? It was obviously worth a great deal more than the simple little dress he had destroyed. They were just not in the same class.

Lee didn't expect that would be the last she would hear of it, though, and she was right. Before she went home that night, Adam appeared in her office, firmly closing the door behind him.

Warily, she looked up to find him regarding her with very nearly no expression on his face. She thought, *at least he doesn't look angry.*

'Don't you like the dress?' he asked. 'Or is it the wrong size?'

'I didn't try it for size,' she said. 'And it doesn't matter if I like it or not. I can't accept it.'

'Can't—or won't?'

'Won't, then.'

'I owe you a dress.'

'So give me a cheque.'

'I thought you wouldn't approve of that.'

'What do you mean?'

'You're the one who accused me of thinking money could fix everything,' he reminded her. 'I spent all morning choosing that dress.'

'You bought it yourself?' Somehow Lee had thought he would have picked up the telephone, or perhaps ordered his secretary to do so, and given her size and his requirements to some anonymous salesperson in a city store.

'I chose it myself,' he confirmed. 'Maybe I should have taken you along. But somehow I didn't think you would come.'

'You were right,' she said. 'I'm sorry it was all for nothing.'

'I was looking forward to seeing you wearing it.'

'It isn't exactly the sort of thing one wears to the office,' she pointed out.

A faint smile flickered across his face. 'I wasn't thinking of the office,' he told her. 'I have an invitation for you—from my father. He was so impressed with your performance on Saturday night, he wants to meet you. My parents have a beach home at Pauanui. They asked me to bring you down for a weekend.'

'That's kind of them, but——'

'Don't turn it down flat,' he said swiftly. 'My father is retired now, and quite old. But he likes to feel he still has a finger in the pie of the business. He was impressed with you on television, and it would give him a great deal of pleasure if you would come.'

Put like that, it would seem unnecessarily selfish and rude not to accept. Reluctantly, Lee asked, 'When?'

'Are you free next weekend?'

'Well—yes, I suppose so.'

'Good. It's his birthday on Saturday. I'll take you home after work and we can drive straight on down on Friday night, if that's all right.'

'I don't want to intrude on a family party——'

'Don't be silly. It'll make his day. There will be a small party on Saturday evening—just family and a few friends. That's when I hoped you would wear the dress.' Adam paused. 'Will you change your mind?'

Resolutely she shook her head.

'Too bad. I'm not going to write you a cheque, you know. It's the dress or nothing.'

'Then I'll settle for nothing, thank you. It's worth at least twice as much as the one you—the other one, anyway.'

'Does that matter?'

'To me, it does.'

'Weren't you ever taught to accept gifts graciously?'

'My upbringing was old-fashioned. Nice girls only accept flowers, books and chocolates from men,' she said lightly, making him smile.

'And giving you a dress might indicate I had designs on your virtue?'

It was on the tip of her tongue to say, *haven't you?* because on last night's showing it certainly seemed possible, and the dress, even in the box, was obviously sexy though not in any loudly vulgar way. But that sounded rather like an invitation, and she didn't want to start anything. Instead she said, 'I know that isn't why you bought it.'

'Thanks for that, anyway,' he drawled. 'It's one villainy you don't credit me with.'

'I don't credit you with any villainy,' she protested. A certain ruthlessness, and some double-dealing as far as women were concerned, but that hardly amounted to anything that might be called villainous.

'Then you won't mind travelling with me on Friday?'

'Of course not. I don't expect a repetition of last night.'

'Don't you?' Adam looked as though he might say more, but Helen tapped on the door, saying, 'I'm off, Lee. Those proofs you wanted are on my desk.'

Adam opened the door. 'It's all right,' he said, nodding pleasantly to Helen as he walked past her. 'We've finished our business.'

'He looks happy today,' Helen remarked as Lee began tidying her desk for the night. 'I guess he's as pleased as the rest of us with the interviews last night.'

Maybe that was why he hadn't been too annoyed at her refusal to accept the dress, Lee thought. He had certainly taken that much better than she had expected.

Afterwards she realised she should have known he would not accept defeat so easily.

She wouldn't let him come in when he drove her to the flat to collect her weekend bag and change from her work clothes into something more casual. She didn't want to be reminded of the last time he had come and she thought that Adam realised it, because he flashed her a mildly sardonic glance and agreed unexpectedly easily to stay in the car and wait for her.

As Lee got out she noticed Mark's Mercedes parked a short way along the street and was obscurely relieved that the two men were not going to meet, without being exactly sure why.

Not only Mark, but two other young men and a dark-haired, plump girl were in the flat with Michael. He was looking slightly flushed and very happy as he asked Lee if she minded his asking a few friends in for a while.

'Of course not, darling!' she assured him. 'I want you to make yourself at home here.'

The boys were Graham and Boris, but the girl interested Lee more. Her name was Janet Crane and she had a vivacious, friendly manner, and a pretty, dimpled-cheeked smile. She was sitting on the sofa next to Michael and while Lee collected last-minute things from her bedroom and hastily brushed her hair and renewed her make-up, she could hear the two of them talking, Michael taking a much greater part in the conversation than usual.

When Lee rejoined Adam in the car and he had stowed her bag in the boot, she sat quiet and thoughtful as he started the car and drove through the streets to the motor-way that would take them south.

The traffic was heavy at this hour and he concentrated on his driving until they were past the inner suburbs and travelling past green, rolling farmland.

Then he commented, 'You're looking thoughtful.'

'I'm sorry I'm not good company,' she said. 'I'm rather tired.'

Slightly impatient, he said, 'I wasn't criticising. I find chatter when I'm driving in heavy traffic rather distracting, actually.' After a pause he added, 'You're welcome to have a nap if you want to. There's a small pillow on the back seat if you want to put it behind your head.'

'Thank you, but I don't need it.'

Lee gazed out at the landscape, watching a couple of horses chasing each other across a paddock, and catching a glimpse of a lone blue-black pukeko stalking across a low swamp on its bright red legs, the thick, short red beak giving it an air of hauteur.

She felt unaccountably depressed, and wanted to break the silence, but could think of nothing to say. She glanced at Adam's profile and found him looking rather grim, his eyes focused on the road ahead, his mouth firm and tight.

'Did you have a bad day?' she asked.

'Would it matter to you if I had?'

He didn't take his eyes off the road, which was as well, because she had to control a sudden urge to cry, holding back stinging tears.

'I'm sorry,' she said stiffly. 'I was just trying to make conversation. I won't chatter any more.'

'Don't be so sensitive. As a matter of fact mine was a perfectly serious question. *Would* it matter to you?'

Everything to do with him mattered. But she wasn't going to tell him that. She said, with a hint of mischief, 'You're driving me tonight, and it's a long way. If you had a bad day it might affect my safety.'

His lightning glance acknowledged her evasion and promised retribution all at once, even though he smiled slightly in appreciation of the put-down. 'Peace!' he said quite mildly. 'As you say, we've a long drive ahead.' He put out his hand and clasped hers briefly. 'Let's put away the weapons for a while, shall we?'

She had never had any adequate weapons against him, anyway. She didn't answer directly but said instead, 'Tell me about your family—who am I going to meet?'

As well as his mother and father there would be two of his sisters there with their husbands, he told her. Gail, the older one, had two children aged four and two; Lisa, the younger sister, had no children, but was married to a well-known radio announcer who was the life and soul of any party. He had a younger brother in America who was also married.

Lee supposed his family would be pleased that he was planning to marry, too. But she didn't say so. The thought skittered into her mind and was firmly ejected.

At Bombay they stopped at one of the fruit and vegetable

shops that were scattered along the roadside, and bought some apples and a big bag of fresh carrots from the market gardens of the Pukekohe hill. The hill itself could be seen in the distance, patchworked with gardens making the most of its rich brown volcanic soil.

'My mother always puts in an order when I'm coming this way,' Adam told her. 'She's a great believer in a bargain.'

Lee smiled, thinking she would see a whole new aspect of him this weekend. She wondered if he was different with his family. And what sort of little boy he had been. Maybe his sisters, and his mother, might talk about his childhood.

But she wasn't a girl he was bringing home in that sense, of course. She was just someone from the office that his father wanted to meet. They would have met Lisbet, of course—the girl he was going to marry.

By the time they reached the Kopu turn-off and began winding up into the Coromandel ranges it was getting towards dusk. The native bush lining the road on either side looked dark and mysterious, and as they entered its shadow, Lee shivered a little.

Adam reached over and switched on the car's heater. The warmth flowed over her toes and rose to encompass her whole body, until she began to feel deliciously drowsy. She shook her head to keep herself awake, and saw that Adam had turned to look at her.

'What's the trouble?' he enquired.

'Just waking myself up,' she said.

'Sleep if you like.'

'No. It makes me dopey, sleeping in a car.'

'Would you like to get out and stretch for a while?'

'Do we have time?'

'All the time in the world.' He drove on a little further and then pulled over into a lay-by.

Lee got out as he was opening his own door, and walked to the edge of the gravel. In front of her the hillside fell away steeply, manuka and native ferns clothing it in dense vegetation. The small white flowers of the manuka bobbed and swayed a little in an evening breeze. In the distance the mountains rolled away, the bush that covered them making them look deeply blue-grey against the pale sky.

The breeze eddied some dust about her feet, and raised goose-pimples on her arms, so that she shivered again and rubbed herself with her hands.

She didn't know Adam was behind her until his jacket dropped about her shoulders. Then she turned to protest, saying, 'There's no need——'

But he was closer than she had realised, his hands still holding the jacket, and when she turned her head and looked into his eyes her voice faltered and died. In the dusk his eyes looked darker and more gentle than she had ever seen them, and when his hands tightened on her shoulders and turned her into his arms she didn't even think of objecting, it seemed so natural.

When his mouth found hers she accepted his kiss willingly, letting the delight of it flow through her as he pressed her closer. One hand still holding the jacket round her, he slipped the other underneath it, lightly stroking her back, the soft curves below, then down to her thighs. Her body flamed into life where he touched her, and his lips on hers were teaching her emotions she had never known before.

She let her arms slip around him, moving her own hands on the hard muscles of his back, and he lifted his mouth for an instant to whisper her name before he took her yearning lips again, almost crushing them with sweet possession.

It was a long time before his mouth lifted again, and she let her arms slide down, her hands resting on his waist. He was looking down at her face with a slight frown and a hint of surprise. His hold on her loosened a little, and she stirred in his arms, faintly alarmed at her own responses. Immediately his hands tightened their grip, not letting her go.

'Lee,' he said huskily, 'I have to tell you ...'

No! her heart cried frantically, and she swiftly raised her hand, stifling his mouth with her fingers. '*Please!* Don't talk, don't say anything!' she begged.

'But, darling——'

'*Don't!*' Almost fiercely she slipped her hand around his neck and pulled his head down again to hers. Her parted lips met his and he gave a surprised little laugh deep in his throat and pulled her close, taking over the kiss until her head bent back over his arm, nudging her legs apart with his thigh so that she knew with a sense of triumph how much he desired her.

A car swept round the bend and uphill, bathing them in sudden light, for it was now nearly dark. Dazzled and suddenly embarrassed, Lee broke away, stepping back until the hard bulk of the car was behind her, grateful that it was almost dark and Adam couldn't see her face clearly.

His jacket had slipped to the ground unnoticed, and he bent and picked it up, dusting it with his hand before he turned towards her. He came over slowly to the car and she fumbled for the door handle, suddenly shy and wanting to turn away. 'We'd better be getting on, hadn't we?' she asked, trying to sound casual and matter-of-fact.

Adam stopped short about three feet away, and her heart thumped uncomfortably.

'Very well,' he said coolly, at last. Lee opened the door and he stood and watched as she climbed into the car, feeling clumsy and not a little foolish. Then he came round and got into the driver's seat. She thought he glanced at her as the automatic light went on, but she wouldn't look at him, and after a moment he closed the door with a small slam, and plunged them into dimness. He started the motor smoothly and switched on the headlamps, and the light reached into the darkness ahead as he brought the car back to the road.

He drove the rest of the way very fast and in total silence. Several times Lee tried to begin a conversation, rolling words around in her mind, but her tongue stuck to her mouth and she couldn't bring herself to actually utter a word. The atmosphere in the car seemed suddenly stifling, and she opened a window a little to let some air in. The night air was cool on her face, and she managed to say carefully, 'Is that too draughty for you?'

Adam shook his head in reply but didn't speak, and she relapsed into silence, not daring to try again, even if she could have thought of something to say.

When they finally arrived at their destination her nerves were stretched to breaking point. She got out without his assistance and stood in the light that spilled from the house, vaguely aware of the salty sea-smell and the distant muted roar of the breakers somewhere out in the darkness.

The door opened and a young woman came out. 'I thought I heard a car,' she exclaimed, coming down the steps to hug Adam briefly. 'Hi, brother. It seems ages since I last saw you.'

'Lee, this is my sister Lisa,' said Adam, turning the girl to face Lee. 'Take her inside, Lisa, while I get the baggage.'

Lisa took her arm in a friendly fashion and guided her into the house. 'I didn't see you on TV,' she said, 'but I believe you were quite a hit. Dad can't wait to meet you.'

In the light Lee could see briefly that Lisa was a little smaller than herself, with blue eyes like her brother's but with a sparkle that his lacked, and thick, glossy brown hair, which fell to her shoulders. She took Lee into a large sitting room and introduced her to Mr and Mrs Broome. Looking with interest at Adam's father, she could see a strong resemblance, although the father's hair had been darker and was now almost entirely grey. His handshake was firm, but she noticed that his movements were slow and he seemed glad to subside again into the armchair he had risen from to greet her.

Mrs Broome was on the plump side and surprisingly motherly-looking. She had her daughter's dark hair, but it was cut quite short in a rather chic modern style.

'You must be tired and hungry,' she said to Lee. 'As soon as Adam brings in your things I'll take you up to your room and once you've freshened up a little come down and I'll get you something to eat.'

Lee's room was small but pretty, and it had a minute bathroom with a shower and toilet built into one corner. She used the bathroom and combed her hair, smoothed down her skirt and descended the wide polished wood stairs.

Adam was waiting for her at the foot of the stairs. He watched her as she came down, and she carefully looked at each step as she descended, avoiding his eyes.

'I'm to show you the way to the kitchen,' he said as she joined him. 'My mother has a meal waiting for us.'

Like the rest of the house the kitchen was very up-to-date and beautiful. Mrs Broome was attending to a casserole in the glass-fronted wall oven, answering Lee's murmured worry about going to a lot of trouble with a cheerful, 'No trouble, dear. We expected you to arrive quite late, so I kept some for you. I hope you like chicken and rice casserole.'

Lee said she was sure she would, and on tasting it at the

small table in the kitchen could say with all sincerity it was delicious. She had half expected to find a housekeeper in charge, because obviously Mr Broome senior had quite a lot of money. But evidently Adam's mother preferred to run her own home, or at least to do the cooking.

She placed two glass bowls in front of them containing chocolate mousse and cream, and then said, 'Well, I'll leave you two to eat in peace. When you've finished you know where to find us all.'

'By the way, where's Tom?' asked Adam, and Lee had the strangest feeling that it was because his mother was leaving the room and he didn't want to be left alone with Lee.

'He just went out to get some cigarettes.' His mother smiled. 'Lisa wants him to give up smoking, so she carefully forgot to include them in the grocery list. It didn't work.'

Adam smiled in return and nodded, and then his mother went out and left the two of them alone.

CHAPTER TEN

'Tom is Lisa's husband, isn't he?' Lee asked to break the silence. 'He's Tom Tripper, the radio announcer?'

'That's right. You'll get the family sorted out as you meet them. You'll meet Gail and Andrew and their two children tomorrow. They're driving up from Tauranga and should be here for lunch.'

'Will they be staying here?'

'No—a mile or so down the coast, at the cottage—we have a smaller place that the family used as a holiday home for years, before Dad retired and built this. It's still available for our use and sometimes loaned to friends. Gail and Andrew prefer to have their family there rather than cram into this when we're all down for a weekend.'

Lee asked about the children and he told her Gail had a girl and a boy, in that order, and their names were Jenny and Shawn.

Lee couldn't think of anything to say, and concentrated on finishing her casserole. She was hungrier than she had realised, and appreciated the chocolate mousse that followed.

Adam got up and made some coffee, then suggested they should drink it in the other room with the family. Lee agreed with alacrity because although the atmosphere had eased a little, she still felt tense with him.

He put the cups on a tray and carried them into the living room, preceding her down the wide hall. Tom had arrived and she was introduced to him, a tall, fair man with

132

an engaging grin and a non-stop tongue which kept her entertained and saved her from having to talk to Adam again all evening.

She went to bed as soon as she decently could, pleading tiredness after the journey, and genuinely nursing the beginning of a headache.

Adam got up and saw her to the foot of the stairs, where she firmly said goodnight, turning away quickly in case he should try to claim a goodnight kiss. That brief madness in the mountains had been all too pleasant, but the implications needed thinking about before she succumbed to temptation again.

'Goodnight, Lee,' said his voice, already behind her as she mounted the stair. 'If you want me—for anything—my door is the one opposite yours.'

Involuntarily she turned to stare at him, and wished that she had had the sense to ignore him instead. He was looking at her, quizzically amused, and waiting for her reaction. When she swung round and continued up the stairs without speaking, he laughed softly and then she heard him returning to the living room.

She woke early in the morning, to the insistent sound of the nearby surf and the intermittent chirping of land birds mingling with the recurring calls of the seagulls.

Lee looked out of the window and saw smooth green lawns and colourful shrubs near the house, with a wide view of the sea beyond. The air was still and the blue water rolling to shore looked lazy and inviting under a pale blue sky.

She fancied a swim, but knew it wasn't wise to swim on a strange beach alone, so she left her red satin bikini in its bag and pulled on a thin knitted cotton shirt with long sleeves and a pair of jeans over tiny bikini panties, and slipped her feet into a pair of thonged sandals. After smoothing on a modicum of lip gloss and a faint trace of eyeshadow and combing her hair, she slipped out of the room.

Adam was leaning against the wall nearby, dressed in casual slacks and a white roll-necked shirt, with a rolled towel under his arm.

'I thought I heard you stirring,' he said. 'I was just about to knock. Like to go for a swim?'

Lee hardly hesitated. 'Just a minute,' she said, and slipped back into her room for a towel and the red bikini. She stuffed them hastily into a cotton macramé bag with a comb and a small make-up sachet, pulled the drawstring top closed and joined Adam.

'Quick,' he said, nodding approval. 'Let's go.'

Outside the house he told her, 'I was going to walk down to the cottage. It's safer swimming there. But if you prefer to ride I'll get out the car.'

'No, let's walk.'

'You're sure?'

'Positive. I like walking in the mornings.'

'Great minds ...' he smiled, and took her arm lightly to steer her across the lawn to an almost hidden path that went steeply downhill towards the sea, winding away from the cultivated garden with its spectacular orange leucospermums and huge trumpets of pink and red hibiscus, into a grove of whispering pines. 'There's a short cut,' Adam explained. 'It's nicer than the road.'

It was, but they had to watch their feet because an occasional root humped itself out of the ground near the pine trees and made a trap for unwary walkers. But after some time the trees thinned and gave way to sand-dunes covered with blue lupins and tussock grass. The sea was visible, curling creamily on to white-gold sand, and the sky had intensified in colour now that the sun was higher in its blue arc. It promised to be a beautiful day.

The cottage, when they reached it, was of an unpretentious weatherboard, only one storey, painted pale blue with white window surrounds and a dark blue front door facing the sea. There were trees around it and the springy buffalo grass felt rough on Lee's bare toes as they crossed it to the door.

Adam opened the door with a key he took from his pocket and waved her inside. She walked directly into a living room with a small kitchenette divided from it by a set of shelves and cupboards. There were two divans built into one corner of the room which obviously could double as beds, and the rest of the furniture looked comfortable and even slightly shabby.

At the other side of the room was a short passageway with a door at the end and one on each side. Adam led her into it and told her, 'That's the bathroom at the end. You can have one of the bedrooms to change in. I'll use the other.'

The room housed only a double bed and a dressing-table with an almost full-length mirror. Lee changed swiftly, suspecting that Adam was dressed for swimming beneath his clothes, and not wanting to keep him waiting. She folded her clothes neatly on the bed and as she turned to leave the room caught a glimpse of herself in the mirror. It wasn't a particularly daring style, but she suddenly felt very bare in the clinging red satin, and decided to pull on her shirt over it. It barely cleared the top of her bikini pants, but she felt more covered, and was able to return to the living room swinging her towel with some nonchalance.

Adam had slung his around his neck and was waiting for her, wearing brief swim shorts in a dark blue colour. He had a good, muscular body that was nicely tanned.

He barely glanced at her before opening the door. They walked in silence down to the beach and Lee realised that they had not spoken much at all this morning. She had been busy absorbing the sights and the atmosphere of the salty morning air and contented to just stroll beside him, pushing aside the thoughts that had troubled her last night. She had lain awake for some time, wondering if the way he had kissed her last night meant anything more than the first time he had done so—because he gave in to an impulse on finding 'a pretty girl' in his arms. It had been almost accidental at first, and she supposed he hadn't really meant it to happen at all. Only she had happened to turn at that particular moment, and proximity and natural biological urges had done the rest. His casual air this morning seemed to indicate that he had not lost any sleep over it, at least. She had been afraid last night that he was about to tell her that he was committed to someone else—*I have to tell you*, he had started to say—and she cringed inwardly as she recalled how she had stopped him, wanting only to enjoy the moment, without spoiling its magic by recalling other obligations—*other loves*.

He stopped on the soft sand above high-water mark and dropped his towel on a convenient driftwood log that lay there half buried. He was waiting for her, watching, and she suddenly wished she had not worn the shirt. The buttoned neckline only reached half-way down the front, and somehow pulling it off in front of him was going to seem far more intimate than simply wearing her bikini from the start. If she turned away or told him to go on she was going to look foolishly prudish.

He was still waiting, the beginning of a smile etching his

mouth as though he was aware of her dilemma.

Defiantly she grasped the edges of the shirt and swiftly pulled it over her head and dropped it beside his towel, shaking her hair out of her eyes. His eyes ran swiftly over the lithe slimness of her body, but he made no comment and began walking towards the water.

It was cold in the sea and when she was thigh-deep she stopped, hugging her arms around herself in trepidation. But there was a roller on the way, and Adam grinned and put his arm around her waist as it reached them, lifting her with him over its crest and then releasing her as they both began swimming.

It was fun diving into the waves, but he was a stronger swimmer than she, and after half an hour she had had enough. The sun was quite warm when she came out, shaking water from her hair, and she sank down on her towel and let it dry out before sitting up to comb out the tangles. She could see Adam's head bobbing up now and then among the breakers, but the only other swimmers were far away along the sandy curve of the beach.

She sat on the driftwood log and rested her arms on her knees, letting her hair fall forward and fan over her shoulders to dry. The sun was warm on her back and she curled her toes sensuously into the soft sand at her feet. The sun's gentle warmth, the muted boom of the waves, the occasional screech of a gull wheeling into the morning air, lulled her into an almost-doze.

A cool, wet finger trailing up her spine made her sit up with a startled gasp.

Adam, still wet from his swim, towel in hand, was smiling down at her. 'And to think I was relying on you to rescue me if I got into trouble!' he said teasingly. 'You're more than half asleep.'

'I wasn't,' she protested, watching him as he towelled his

body dry. 'Anyway, you're a better swimmer than I am. You're hardly likely to need rescuing.'

He slung the towel about his neck again and sat beside her, but facing the other way on the log. He studied her face and said lazily, 'You look rather sweet when you're sleepy. I can imagine you first thing in the morning when you've just woken up.'

'Do you think so?' she enquired with cool scepticism.

'I do,' he said softly. 'Shall I put it to the test?'

As she turned fully to face him, wondering if she should be angry, he added, 'I could come and wake you tomorrow morning—if you'd like to swim again.'

'I don't think that will be necessary,' said Lee, standing up without haste. He was teasing and she wasn't going to let him provoke her into any but the coolest reaction.

Adam turned on the log, straddling it, and watched as she picked up her comb and dropped it into the macramé bag and tied the sleeves of her shirt around her neck in a loose knot. She wasn't going to put it on again in front of him.

'Do you want to go?' he asked.

'Won't we be expected?' she hedged.

'For breakfast? Not necessarily. Breakfast is when you want it at weekends. We could have it here at the cottage if you like. There'll be supplies in the kitchen.'

Lee didn't reply to that, and apparently taking her silence for consent, Adam stood up and took her hand in his saying, 'Come on. I'll cook while you change.'

In the bedroom she rolled her bikini in the towel after drying herself and slipped on her jeans and shirt and combed her hair again. As she slung her bag over her shoulder to leave the room and glanced in the mirror she realised that it was fairly obvious she wasn't wearing a bra, and while that was certainly not considered indecent these days, she wished she had taken the time to put one on this morning. She thought of replacing the top of her bikini, but that was damp and might only make matters worse. After all, Adam's manner this morning had been so casual it bordered on the impersonal. He was a fairly sophisticated man and hardly likely to turn into a sex maniac at the sight of her barely covered breasts. Even when he had put his arm about her briefly in the water, when the two of them had been very nearly naked, he had released her almost immediately, obviously not stirred at all. Last night she knew she had aroused him, but he had accepted it when she called a halt, and simply not mentioned the episode since. She supposed that for him it was simply a pleasant but unimportant little interlude in the monotony of the long drive.

She emerged to find him standing over the stove, still wearing his swimsuit. Barely glancing at her, he said, 'Everything's either frozen or tinned. You can have bacon with baked beans, spaghetti or tinned corn.'

'I like baked beans,' she said. 'But I'm not fussy if you prefer one of the others.'

'Baked beans it is,' he said, reaching for the tin from a shelf nearby, and taking a tin-opener from a drawer. A delicious smell of frying bacon rose from the pan on the stove, and Lee realised she was hungry.

Dropping her bag on the divan in the corner, she asked, 'What can I do?'

'Make some toast from that sliced bread, if you will,' said Adam, indicating a wrapped sliced loaf lying on the small workbench. 'The toaster is right there.'

He removed the bacon and put it on plates, placing them in the warmer at the bottom of the stove, then tipped in the baked beans, turning down the heat and putting a lid on the pan. 'That'll be right for a while,' he said, and went into the bedroom where he had left his clothes.

When he emerged again he had donned his slacks but not his shirt. His still damp hair looked darker than usual, and his brown chest had a sparse vee of the same colour in the middle that disappeared into the waistline of his pants. He looked extraordinarily handsome, and Lee remembered with surprise that when she first met him she had thought him unremarkable.

She had made two pieces of toast, prising the slices of frozen bread apart with a knife, but the butter was frozen too, and she was trying to scrape some off the top of the block without much success.

'Here,' said Adam, taking a cheese slicer from the drawer, and grasping the butter firmly he soon had several thin slices which he proceeded to place on the toast, where they melted deliciously.

'Mmm, male ingenuity,' Lee murmured, mock-admiring, wondering if he remembered his own reference to the female variety. 'No wonder you're a top executive!'

He cast her an amused glance and said, 'I'm also very good at giving orders. Set the table—you'll find everything handy.'

'Yes, sir—certainly, sir,' she said meekly, and set to work.

He made a derisive sound and said, 'You can't fool me, you know. I've never met anyone less inclined to obey orders than you.'

'*I've* never met anyone more prone to giving them,' she returned smartly, as she removed some knives and forks from the drawer.

As always, she was unprepared for the swiftness of his reactions. As she turned to continue laying the table, he grabbed her wrists and pulled her to him, dropping a swift, hard kiss on her surprised mouth. He released her immediately, saying, 'Now behave yourself, Miss Palmer, or I'll silence you for a good deal longer than that!'

He was smiling, and suddenly her heart was singing. They had never been lighthearted with each other before, and she loved it—she loved *him*. Just for this one moment out of their lifetimes she could pretend that he loved her too.

She made a face and returned to her task, smiling as she heard his soft laughter behind her.

He opened a can of orange juice, and then, inspecting the contents of the refrigerator, exclaimed, 'Aha! Just what we need,' and withdrew a bottle of sparkling white wine.

'For breakfast?' queried Lee, laughing.

'Why not? What's wrong with a champagne breakfast?' Adam found two stemmed glasses in a cupboard and placed them on the table. So they had both orange juice and the wine, and Lee decided it was quite the best meal she had ever had in her life. Breakfast must surely be the most intimate meal of the day, and it was easy to pretend for a few minutes that this was not their first and last breakfast together.

They followed the baked beans and bacon with marmalade on toast, and then Adam made coffee. 'Black, or the coffee'n'milk variety?' he asked, holding up two jars of instant coffee for her choice. Lee asked for black, and was idiotically pleased when he opted for the same, showing their tastes coincided in this small way.

They lingered over the coffee, talking about work and then about a variety of other things, and occasionally sharing a joke. Lee had let him give her two glasses of the wine, and she felt a little lightheaded as well as lighthearted. The coffee sobered her a bit, but she sang softly to herself as they did the dishes together. After a while Adam began to whistle in harmony, and she didn't remember when she had been so happy.

He went to collect his things from the bedroom, and she sat on the divan, looking out of the window at the sunlit sea.

She went on looking as she heard him come back into the room, because she was suddenly shy of what might be in her eyes if she looked at him. But when he came over to the divan she sighed a little and reached for her bag, knowing the little interlude was over and they would have to return to the real world.

He had his towel under his arm and his shirt hooked over his shoulder on his fingers, but as she made to pick up her bag and rise from the divan, he leaned over to get it for her at the same time. There was a soft collision, and he dropped his shirt and towel, grabbing her about the waist to steady her.

She found her face against his bare shoulder, her hands holding his arms to keep her balance. He didn't move his hands from her waist, and when she raised her eyes he was looking at her with a question in his. She could have said no. She knew that, even as she felt him shift his feet to take her weight against him, even as his mouth descended quite slowly to hers. She could have said no, but she didn't. Instead she let her hands slide up his arms to his shoulders, caressingly, and then link around his neck, as he continued to kiss her, a long, slow, sensuous kiss that made her feel warm and weightless all over.

His hands went under her shirt and began moving against the smooth skin of her back, and as his mouth left hers she slid her fingers into his hair and arched her throat, encouraging him to explore its curving line with his lips, from the slight hollow beneath her ear to the shadow between her breasts where the neckline of her shirt brought him to a halt. She whispered his name and he raised his head and kissed her mouth again, until she felt almost faint with desire for him.

She didn't protest when he gently lowered her to the divan, his mouth still seductively on hers, his hands on her back still pressing her close to his bare chest, only the thin material of her shirt separating them, as he lay with her, his thighs pressing against hers.

Briefly she opened her eyes and saw him, as he raised his lips from hers, looking into her face with a concentrated, intent gaze, and she realised that one of his hands had shifted its grip on her back and was sliding over her rib cage to her breast, gently cupping its softness. Her eyes involuntarily widened a little with shocked surprise, and the ghost of a smile crossed his mouth before he brought it down again to her parted lips, stilling any slight protest she might have made and drawing a passionate response from her.

Then his lips left hers and he seemed to lift himself a little away from her, the warmth of his hand on her body slipping away. She opened her eyes as a slight coolness made itself felt on her midriff and saw his bent head and felt his hands on the bottom of her shirt, pushing it up.

'*No!*' She stiffened suddenly beneath him and frantically grabbed at his wrists, pushing them down.

He looked up and she could see a faint flush under his tan and the glitter of desire in his eyes. He smiled a little at her sudden panic and bent to kiss the hollow of her throat, exploring it with his tongue. In spite of herself Lee relaxed a little, but her hands still held his wrists, and when he began again to ease her shirt up, she tightened her grip and said, 'Adam, please—no!'

He raised his head and looked into her eyes. 'Darling, please—*yes*!' he said, and behind the gentle mockery was a hint of real pleading. 'You're so beautiful—I want to see you, I want to feel you close to me, your lovely soft skin against mine.' His voice was husky with passion, and she wanted to give in, but she knew this was the point of no return, and that if she let him have his way her own passion would be beyond her control.

She swallowed and said, 'No.' Her nails dug into his wrists as she tried to wriggle away from him. 'Let me go!'

Their eyes clashed as he saw that she meant it, and she could see he was tempted to force the issue, knowing that she was likely to surrender if he used his superior strength to hold her in his arms until her own desire overcame her scruples.

'*No*, Adam,' she said softly, her eyes begging him to play fair, to leave her self-respect intact. 'No more. That's enough.'

'Enough?' he asked with soft derision. But he rolled away from her and stood up in one swift, fluid motion. He picked up his towel and re-rolled it, then slung his shirt over his shoulder again while she quickly attempted to tidy her hair, sitting on the edge of the divan.

She gathered up her bag and straightened the rumpled shirt, and stood up.

Adam was standing in front of her, one hand hooked into the belt of his pants, his look coolly reflective. 'Do you often do that?' he asked abruptly.

'Do what?'

'Let a man kiss you like that—then say, "enough".'

Wordlessly Lee shook her head, and turned blindly towards the door. But he got there before her, and stopped with his hand on the knob.

'At least this time,' he said, 'you won't pretend that I leave you cold.'

It took some courage, but she managed to raise her eyes and look full at him. 'No,' she said, 'I won't pretend that.'

For a long moment he held her eyes with his, and then he gave a small nod, as though her answer had satisfied him, or he had scored some point. Then he twisted the doorknob and let her pass by him into the open air.

CHAPTER ELEVEN

LEE spent most of the afternoon talking to Adam's father. Gail and her husband, Richard Evans, had arrived just before lunch with the two children, and Lee had been amused and a little surprised to notice that 'Uncle Adam' was obviously a favourite with them. Their father and Adam were persuaded to play with them on the back lawn while Gail joined the other adults on the wide wooden terrace overlooking the ocean. Mr Broome got Lee to sit beside him and soon had her telling him all about her job and the new magazine—or the new style of the old one.

He had a very good grasp of the basic information already, and she realised that Adam must have been keeping him well informed.

'I believe that you write, too,' he said, startling her with the knowledge.

'A little,' she admitted.

'And very well, according to my son,' her companion told her.

Lee wondered just how much she had been discussed. As though guessing at her thoughts, Mr Broome added, 'I was impressed with you on that television programme. I pumped him about you.'

'I see.'

'He didn't know much about your personal life, though.'

'I don't talk much about my personal life at work,' Lee answered.

'Do you have a family?'

'Only my mother and one brother. *Your* family is fortunate. Do you often get together like this?'

He smiled a little grimly, reminding her of his son, and said, 'Not so often nowadays. It's nice when it's possible.'

'Do you hear from your son in America much?'

'He writes often. You've been asking a few questions, too, haven't you?'

'I wanted to know who I would be meeting. Naturally Adam mentioned the brother who would be absent this weekend.'

As the talk flowed on, he didn't try to probe her private life again, although she felt that if he had really been interested he would have persevered. He wasn't the sort of man to give up easily if something mattered to him. Lee liked him, and the rest of Adam's family. But she didn't want them to start looking on her as anything other than a business colleague of Adam's. Their family circle was an attractive one, but it would only hurt her to be drawn into it.

She tried not to think about the events of the morning, finding the memory too confusing. She felt she should be ashamed of her weakness in letting Adam make love to her, but could not hide from herself her longing for him to do it again. She tried to despise him for kissing her when all the signs pointed to his being committed elsewhere. She listened hopefully to an inner voice that said perhaps he *wasn't*—that she had been mistaken, and all the love was on Lisbet's side. But he had broken a date to see Lisbet, and not only Lisbet but her family obviously regarded him as hers. It had been obvious to even an outsider. Brian, too, had foreseen imminent wedding bells for them.

And if Adam was going to marry Lisbet, why did he persist in making love to Lee?

Later, as she got out her flowered skirt and grey blouse for the evening's celebration, Lee thought of several plausible and rather depressing reasons. Proximity, for one. Adam had given her to understand almost as soon as they met that he was susceptible to a pretty face and willing to take advantage of it if the opportunity presented itself. He had never made any secret of the fact that he found her attractive.

He wouldn't be the first man to want to have his cake and eat it, too. So far, to her knowledge, he wasn't even officially engaged, so no doubt he felt it was permissible to have some sort of fling before the knot was finally tied. And she had to admit that she had not exactly repulsed him this time. At least, not at first.

She stripped and shut herself into the tiny bathroom for her shower, glancing down at the neat, firm figure that she had finally denied him the sight of this morning, glad for her pride's sake that she had done so, but with a hidden undercurrent of regret.

She turned the water on full and closed her eyes against its stinging warmth, trying to think of nothing, without success. A sickening thought came into her head, choking her throat, that maybe Adam was simply still bent on disproving her earlier assertions that she was indifferent to him. She realised that subconsciously she had been hoping that he simply couldn't help himself, that maybe, in spite of the evidence of his attachment to Lisbet, he would discover he loved *her* instead, that a little encouragement might make him admit it.

Idiotic, adolescent dreams! Adam had never suggested that his desire for her contained any element of love. He was quite frank about 'wanting' her, but that certainly had little to do with the reality of love, the kind that grew better with age and time, the kind that real marriages were made of. And Lee knew that was the only kind of value to her, not for the piece of paper that meant respectability and a legal tie, but for the commitment to lifelong loving that it implied. At heart she was a pretty old-fashioned girl.

Well, she had certainly given him some encouragement so far this weekend, but the more she thought about it, the more she was oppressed by the horrible feeling that all it meant to him was a satisfying of his conviction that she 'felt something' for him, even if it wasn't love, a vindication of his ability to conquer her bravely asserted aversion.

The trouble was, it was absolutely no use now pretending any more that she hated him to touch her, or even that she didn't care one way or the other. She had let him see all too clearly how he affected her physically.

But if the whole thing was a cruel game to him—it was one that two could play. By the time Lee stepped from the shower she had her strategy mapped out.

When she stepped from the bathroom, followed by a whiff of steam and scented talcum powder, she stopped short, shaking her head. She must be mistaken.

But she wasn't. Spread out on the bed in place of the skirt and blouse she had left there was the golden-tan dress that she had returned to Adam's office the other day. There was also a very filmy, very glamorous notion of a jacket which obviously went with it, the sort of thing which suggested modesty without hiding anything at all.

Coming on top of her late cogitations, it was too much. She flung open the door of the wardrobe in the corner, took a quick look inside her small suitcase, and hardly stopping to tie the belt of her towelling robe, marched across the passageway outside her room to rap sharply on the door opposite.

Adam's voice called to her to come in, and she did, shutting the door behind her with a decisive snap.

He was just putting on a shirt, and hardly paused while his fingers did up the buttons.

'What have you done with my clothes?' Lee demanded.

'I haven't touched them.' He flickered a slightly amused glance over her tousled, damp-ended hair and the hastily tied robe. Leaving his top button undone, he began tucking the shirt into his dark pants.

'That's a pretty stupid lie!' she stormed. 'You're surely not going to tell me you don't know what I'm talking about.'

He finished what he was doing, then stood facing her, his thumbs hooked into his belt, feet slightly apart on the carpet. 'It isn't a lie. And no, I won't say I don't know what you're talking about.'

'That hardly follows, does it?'

'Doesn't it?'

Getting madder by the minute, she took a couple of steps towards him. 'I'm not wearing that dress,' she told him forcefully. 'So you might as well get my own clothes back from wherever you've hidden them and give them back to me.'

'I can't. I don't know where they are.'

'I'm sure you could easily find out,' she said, with almost gritted teeth, trying to control her temper. She wondered if he had got his sister or perhaps his mother to be his accomplice. She was going to look rather foolish going from room to room asking for her clothes—in front of their husbands, too. Somehow she had to make Adam comply.

He was smiling at her and if she hadn't been so furious with him it would have melted her right away. 'It's a beautiful dress,' he said persuasively. 'Don't you think so?'

'That isn't the point! It's a beautiful bribe——' she added bitterly.

'*What?*'

She started at the whiplash crack of his voice, saying nothing. The smile had left his face and he looked forbidding. 'Must I remind you that I owed you a dress?' he snapped.

'I'd like to remind *you* that it's a much more expensive dress than the one you owed me for.'

'Call it a bonus, then,' he said in almost bored tones. 'I was pleased with your—performance that night.'

The small pause, the mocking gleam in his eyes, convinced her that he was implying a double meaning, and her fury did the rest.

He must have been prepared for the upward swing of her hand, and sidestepped the blow neatly, catching at her wrist as she rocked off balance with her own momentum, and before she could recover he had pulled her down on the bed—*his* bed—and was containing her infuriated struggles with hard, strong fingers and the warm weight of his body on hers.

'If you don't let me go I'll scream!' she threatened, panting in his grasp. His grip only tightened, and she opened her lips, but before she could make a sound he covered them with his, taking full advantage of her parted mouth in a brief but devastating kiss.

His mouth lifted a little and moved across her skin to just below her ear. 'So, scream,' he said. 'And when they all coming running, tell them why you came to my room dressed in next to nothing——?'

She made an inarticulate, furious sound and he lifted his head to look down at her, making her aware that her struggles had loosened the robe she was wearing so that its edges were falling away, almost exposing her breasts.

'You *are* wearing next to nothing, aren't you?' drawled Adam, his voice deep with amusement and something else

—something much more dangerous. 'Have you got *anything* under that?'

Lee didn't answer, making a frantic effort to free her hands from his grasp on her wrists and cover herself. The only notice he took of that was to transfer them easily into one hand, while the other wandered inside the edge of her robe, tracing a burning line from neck to waist, resting on the loose knot of the tie belt as he said, 'Maybe I'll find out for myself,' his eyes following the movement of his hand.

'*Stop it!*' she cried in a choking whisper. 'Adam, *don't*!'

He raised his eyes to hers, holding them almost sternly. 'Will you wear the dress?'

'No!' Rebellion was rife in her voice, until she felt his fingers, very purposeful, on her belt, and she capitulated. '*Yes!* You *beast*! I *hate* you!'

'After this morning,' he said, 'do you expect me to believe that?'

A gentleman wouldn't have mentioned it, she was sure, but then Adam had never been especially polished with her.

His hand had moved from her waist up over the soft curve covered by the towelling and gently pulled at her hair as she tried to think of a way to answer him. 'This morning,' she said finally, 'I was in the mood for a little— necking, that's all. And this morning you weren't *forcing* yourself on me!'

'And I am now?'

'You know you are!'

A very odd expression crossed his face, and he quite abruptly released her and rolled off the bed, so suddenly that she just lay there for a second or two, slightly stunned.

'You're free,' he reminded her quietly, and as she stood up and straightened the robe he crossed to the door and opened it with exaggerated politeness. Lee walked past him without looking into his eyes.

If she had held any hope that the dress would be unwearable it was doomed to an early death. The material was a slightly stretchy modern fabric and from the skimpy folds that covered—just barely—her bust, it skimmed her waist flatteringly before flaring to the floor. The filmy little jacket didn't hide any more than she had expected, but it did, deceptively, make the dress look suitable for a family party.

When she came down and stood on one of the hand-woven natural wool rugs scattered across the wood parquet, waiting for the family to notice her presence and indicate where she should sit, Lisa was the first to greet her, but she had seen Adam turn and silently approve with a comprehensive, sweeping glance before Lisa reached her side.

'It is lovely!' Lisa smiled, with an air of pride that left her in little doubt of the identity of Adam's accomplice. Lee wondered what on earth sort of reason Adam could have given his sister for having bought it, and decided it might be better not to enquire.

'Can I have my skirt back in the morning?' she asked somewhat drily. 'I know it isn't in this class, but it's useful and I'm really quite fond of it.'

Lisa grinned. 'I'll bring it back first thing. I must say, though, my brother has surprisingly good taste!'

Her husband called across, asking Lee what she would like to drink, and as he was pouring her a sherry, Gail arrived with her family.

Lee slipped into a straight chair beside Mrs Broome and sipped slowly at her drink as the family chatter ebbed and flowed. Adam didn't come very near her at all, and she was fairly glad of it. He was disturbing enough even a distance.

Even when Mrs Broome slipped out to put the finishing touches to the rather special meal she was preparing Adam remained standing in a corner, talking to Gail's husband, and it was four-year-old Jenny who ensconced herself on the end of the sofa next to Lee, wriggling her small bottom back against the cushions and carefully balancing a half-glass of lemonade in one hand.

Lee smiled at the child and admired her dress, obviously new for the party, and for a few minutes they carried on an amicable conversation. Jenny was a little honey, Lee decided, before they all repaired to the dining room for roast chicken and apple pie with cream followed by the entrance, ceremonially carried by Mrs Broome and escorted by Shawn and Jenny, of an iced birthday cake.

It was, they said, for the children's enjoyment, but the adults cheered just as loudly when Mr Broome disposed of all the candles with one blow.

Lee insisted on helping Gail with the washing-up, while Lisa put away with Jenny's help. By common consent Mrs Broome had been banished to the sitting room with the men. Adam had a nice family, Lee thought. He himself seemed less hard when they were around him.

Gail and Richard and the children left quite early so that the children were not kept out of bed too late. Shawn had refused to go and sleep on someone's bed, but had succumbed against his father's shoulder some time ago, but Jenny was still lively and protested that she wasn't tired even while her parents were saying goodbye.

'What about the earring?' she demanded, resisting her mother's hold on her small hand.

'Oh, yes, I forgot about it,' Gail exclaimed, hunting in her bag. 'The children found this in the bedroom at the cottage,' she added, holding out a small, glittering object to Lee. 'We presume it's yours, as Adam said you were both down there this morning. And I don't suppose it's his.'

Lee took it automatically, but knew she had been wearing no earrings. It was an expensive-looking one, a pendant of small sapphires, and definitely not hers.

'No, it isn't mine,' she said.

'Not?' Gail was puzzled. 'Well, I wonder who—it isn't yours, is it, Lisa?'

'Let me see,' said Mrs Broome as her other daughter shook her head. 'It's probably Lisbet's. She stayed in the cottage for a few days recently. Or—let me see—did the Tremains use it after that—we lent it to them for a barbecue. Adam——' she turned to her son, 'what date was it that Lisbet was here with——'

'The seventeenth,' he said immediately. 'From the seventeenth to the twenty-first.'

'Oh, yes. Well, that was after the Tremains' barbecue. Do you recognise it?' she asked, passing the earring to him.

'Yes, I believe I have seen her wearing this,' he said, slipping it into his pocket. 'I'll see she gets it back.'

Those dates included the Friday night she had seen him with Lisbet at the theatre, Lee realised. They also encompassed the four days he had been away from the office. Had he stayed with his parents while Lisbet occupied the cottage—or had they shared it?

She turned away and sat down on the sofa, where Mrs Broome joined her after Gail and the family had finally left.

'Do you know Lisbet Carson?' she asked Lee.

'I've met her once or twice,' Lee said evenly, wishing to discuss anything else in the world.

'She's a very nice girl, and she's had a rough time of it. But things seem to be coming right for her at last—

thanks to Adam, I'm pleased to say.' Her eyes strayed affectionately to her son across the room, while Lee tried valiantly to control her expression.

'I'm glad of that,' she managed to say in a barely audible voice. 'I always thought she seemed a nice person.'

She was suddenly very angry with Adam, who had no right to treat either herself or Lisbet the way he did. Lisbet had been hurt enough through her broken marriage, and with a sense of shame that she had ever welcomed Adam's kisses, Lee decided that she had definitely done so for the very last time.

On Sunday it rained and she had no problem avoiding being alone with Adam, because the whole family was confined to the house. They drove back to Auckland together in the late afternoon, and Lee managed to make conversation which passed the time while keeping things on a distantly friendly level. Once or twice he cast her a sharp glance, but seemed content on the whole to follow her lead. It was was with a sense of relief that she left him when he dropped her off at the flat.

She walked in on almost the same scene she had left. Mark was there, and the three young people who had been there on Friday evening.

'Hello,' she said. 'Did you all stay the weekend?'

Amid laughter, they said no, but they had all been out this afternoon, to a concert held at the university, and Michael had invited them back.

They would have gone, but Lee, looking at Michael's slightly flushed pleasure in being accepted as one of the crowd, invited them to stay while she opened some packets and tins and contrived to make a modest meal. Afterwards they sat around talking for ages, and when the telephone rang a lively but goodnatured argument was being conducted in the background as Lee lifted the receiver to hear Adam's voice.

'Are you having a party?' he asked.

'Sort of,' she said, laugher in her voice, because the argument had been a fairly witty one and she was enjoying it. 'Why did you ring?'

'I found something of yours in my car,' he said. 'A small leather purse.'

'Are you sure it's mine?' she asked, tempted to add, *not Lisbet's?*

'White leather, embossed with gold in an oriental design.'

'Oh. Yes, it is mine.'

'I can bring it round if you like.'

'Thank you, but it'll keep until tomorrow.'

'Right, I'll see you then. Enjoy your party.'

'Thanks for ringing.'

'Not at all.' He put down the receiver before Lee had a chance to return his 'Goodnight.'

When they had all gone she helped Michael to open out his bed from the sofa.

'Did you know I could drive a normal car if it had an automatic gearshift?' he asked. 'With a few adjustments that would cost less than two hundred dollars.'

'Could you?' Lee straightened. 'You mean you don't need a special car?'

'Boris is an engineering student. He's done some work for the disabled citizens crowd, and he says it's definitely on.'

An idea which had been forming in Lee's mind for some weeks now took definite shape.

'Mark's going to teach me in his Merc,' said Michael.

'It's an automatic transmission. It'll be a while before I have my own,' he added. 'But it won't hurt to know how, anyway.'

'It certainly won't,' Lee concurred, silently thinking that if she had anything to do with it—and she did intend to have quite a lot, actually—it might not be so very long at all.

CHAPTER TWELVE

LEE had been in her office for an hour or so when Adam came in the following day, dropping the purse on her desk.

'Thank you,' she said, picking it up and placing it in her top drawer. 'I don't know how I came to lose it.'

'Did you enjoy your weekend?'

'Very much. Didn't I make that clear last night?'

'You were very polite and proper last night. You said all the right things. I just didn't know if you meant them.'

Very calm and cool, she said, 'Of course I meant them. I enjoyed meeting your father, and the rest of your family. It was a very pleasant weekend.'

'What about Saturday morning? Would you call that "pleasant" too?'

'Saturday morning?' Lee kept her face blankly enquiring.

'When I took you swimming,' he said with deliberation. 'And afterwards, although it seems to have slipped your memory, you made an exception to your rule of keeping the boss at a safe distance. If you want it spelled out, I made love to you—and you reciprocated.'

Lee shrugged, hoping she looked faintly bored. 'A few kisses,' she said indifferently. 'It hardly comes under the heading of "making love" these days, does it?'

'A little more than a few kisses,' he argued. 'What heading *would* you put it under, then?'

'Under the heading of pleasant memories,' she said, reaching for a file. Glancing up at him she added, 'I shouldn't have broken my rule, I suppose, but we did seem a long way from work, and I enjoyed our swim and the breakfast. It just seemed a nice way to round off the morning. So please don't read any more into it, will you? I thought you would understand.'

'Understand?' Almost she quailed before the cold fury in his face. 'I couldn't *begin* to understand a woman like you, Lee. I'd dearly like to give you something to file under "*un*pleasant memories", and if you ever play a trick like that again, I might just do it!' He turned to leave, stopping with his hand on the door handle to say with soft menace, 'So just watch yourself, won't you?'

The special edition of *Lady* hit the bookstalls, and was very nearly sold out—a resounding success. It looked as though Adam's policy was going to pay off, and the next week's performance supported that optimistic view. Though not quite so high, the sales had risen considerably, and it seemed certain that they would soon be challenging the top seller in the field.

Lee supposed that Adam must be pleased, but the face he presented to her these days was so shuttered and mask-like that she could only guess at his emotions. She scarcely saw him alone, anyway, and he never came to her office. Occasionally she received a summons from his secretary if he wanted to see her, but usually any discussion between them involved another member of the staff as well, or a group meeting.

She should have been pleased that he had stopped tormenting her with his mockery of love-making, but instead she lived with a distant ache behind the film of ice which she had carefully cultivated over her feelings.

Pat Blyth invited her for a meal, and showed her numerous photographs she had taken on her Pacific cruise. Looking at pictures of palm-tree-lined beaches and dark girls with hibiscus blossoms tucked into their hair, Lee had a sudden urge to follow Pat's example and get away from everything for a time—especially from Adam Broome.

'It seems to have done you good,' she commented, noting that Pat looked younger with a fresh tan and a new hairdo.

'I think I've been in a rut,' Pat smiled. 'Adam Broome has done me more than one good turn.'

Lee was puzzled, and showed it.

'I start a new job next Monday,' Pat told her. 'Editing a handcraft publication for one of those firms that specialises in putting out encyclopaedias and handbooks in weekly parts. I'm going to enjoy it. I'm not supposed to know, but I did find out that the job was offered to me on Adam's recommendation.'

So Adam had exerted himself to help Pat, after all. Lee was surprised and obscurely pleased about it. Perhaps he was not quite the hard, unfeeling businessman that he pretended.

Michael's birthday was drawing close, and Lee's plans were well laid. She had enlisted the help of Michael's new friends, and on the morning of his birthday was able to persuade him to go downstairs to the street with her, where she proudly steered him to a new, shiny blue car with a huge birthday card tucked behind the windshield wiper.

After the first shock of surprise his gratitude was boundless.

'How did you do it?' he stammered, sitting behind the wheel and caressing it lovingly with shaking fingers.

'Sold mine,' she said, grinning at him as he turned a face of dismay. 'I hardly used it, anyway, except to visit Mum. Now *you* can drive *me* at weekends instead. It's all ready to go, you know. Boris has fixed it for you.'

She gave a party for him that night, inviting Mark and telling Janet Crane to pass the word to other friends from the university. There were twelve people, boys and girls, in the end, and they had a mildly riotous time. Janet spent a lot of time sitting by Michael and talking to him, and Lee hoped that it wasn't pity that made her do it, because he showed all the signs of being quite smitten.

She had more than one reason to be glad that Michael now had his own transport. Mark had been growing more persistent in his attentions lately, and she, guiltily aware that she had encouraged him considerably at first, was beginning to realise that no amount of trying was going to make him mean half as much to her as Adam. It was irrational and unfair, but there it was.

He followed her into the kitchen where she had gone to check on some savouries heating in the oven, and caught her around the waist as she straightened in front of the stove.

'Mmm, you smell good,' he told her, nuzzling behind her ear with his lips.

Lee broke away from his hold, pinning a smile to her face as she turned. 'Thank you,' she said lightly.

He reached for her again, drawing her into his arms. She stiffened a little, not because it was unpleasant, but because she was afraid of what he might have been reading into her acceptance of his kisses lately.

Mark frowned down at her troubled face. 'What's the matter?'

Lee shook her head. 'Nothing. Only—don't take too much for granted, will you, Mark?'

'What does that mean? Do I have to ask for permission before I put my arms round you?'

Lee shook her head. 'I just meant that—well, we're good friends, Mark. I like you, and I'm very grateful for what you've done for Michael. And I'd like us all to stay—friends.'

His hands fell away from her and she saw that he was angry.

'I think I see,' he said, then laughed a little bitterly. 'I told you I had an ulterior motive for being nice to young Mike. I suppose it serves me right—you've been nice to me to keep me sweet, haven't you? Now he doesn't need me any more—he's got a car and other friends of his own age group, and even a girl. So big sister can give me the push.'

'Oh, Mark! That isn't true!'

'Oh, don't worry, Lee. I admit I wouldn't have been so keen to see so much of your brother if the deal hadn't included you. He's a good kid, but I'd soon have got tired of playing the knight errant. I'm rather glad he's more or less off my hands. He'll be off yours soon, too, I hear.'

'What?' Her head reeling with this new and rather un-attractive side of Mark, she had no idea what he meant.

'Didn't you know the gang have invited him to join them—Boris and Janet and some of the others share an old house in Ponsonby. They've invited Michael to move in.'

'I didn't know.'

'I suppose he'll tell you eventually. As a matter of fact, I had half an idea that when he moved out I might persuade you to share my flat with me. No go, I suppose?'

'No.'

'Pity. Never mind, I'll find someone else.'

He would, too, she didn't doubt. He was good-looking and charming enough, and she suddenly realised that per-haps his emotions were fairly shallow. His kisses had been mostly of the comfortably undemanding sort and he was giving no indication, in spite of his anger, that he really cared deeply about her feelings for him. And she didn't think that he was acting.

He wandered back to the party and later left with one of the girls, a small blonde who was obviously struck by his good looks and who Lee hoped would pour some balm on his wounded pride. For she was convinced that was all it was.

The telephone rang the next morning as she was preparing breakfast for herself and Michael. As she lifted the receiver she saw him struggling to fold up the sofa-bed; his clumsy, one-handed effort made him pant with exertion.

'Michael darling! *I'll* make the bed,' she assured him, flicking her hair out of the way to place the receiver to her ear and say, 'Hello?'

'Is *darling* Michael *living* with you?' Adam's voice snarled in her ear.

Nettled by his tone, she snapped back, '*Yes*. If it's any of your business.'

While it was dawning on her that she had never mentioned her brother to him, and the implication he might take from her reply, he said curtly, 'It isn't, of course. I apologise.' And as she was taking a breath he went on ruthlessly, 'My parents are coming up to town for the day. They asked me to invite you to lunch with us. My father insisted I should ring you first thing and make sure you can come.'

'Well—I don't know,' she said hesitantly, and he snapped, 'Don't be so coy. Yes or no? And I might remind you the invitation isn't mine.'

So he didn't want her to come, and the thought stabbed

at her. Perversely, she said, 'Yes, then. And thank you for passing on the invitation so—graciously.'

She wasn't sure if the sound he made was a laugh, before he said, 'I'll pick you up from your office,' and put down the receiver.

He hardly spoke to her when he came for her, passing a lightning-swift glance over the green dress she had decided to wear, with no sign of recognition. The stain had cleaned out of it and it was the best thing Lee had suitable for a fancy lunch. As she had suspected, they lunched expensively and well, and the conversation of his parents veiled Adam's almost total lack of it.

They were lingering over coffee, although Adam had almost finished his, when Mrs Broome said, 'Oh, look who's just come in,' and Lee's heart plunged as she obediently looked. Lisbet Carson was crossing the room behind a waiter, and with her was a man who looked vaguely familiar.

Both of them smiled as they passed the table, with a quick greeting. The waiter seated them in a corner table for two, and Lee, glancing at Adam, could see no sign of any emotion on his face. She looked again at the couple in the corner and saw Lisbet smiling into the man's face, then caught her breath as she realised who he was.

'That's her husband!' she exclaimed aloud.

'Yes,' Mrs Broome agreed, beaming. 'Isn't it lovely?' Catching the bewilderment in Lee's face, she added, 'You said you know Lisbet, didn't you, Lee?'

'Slightly. But I understood she was divorced——'

'Oh, yes, she was. But they're planning to remarry. Scott came over from America a few weeks ago and finally persuaded her to try again. This time they'll both be older and wiser, and I think it will work out. I think they're really very much in love.'

'Stop gossiping, Mother,' Adam interrupted lazily. Lee's eyes flew to his, but she could read nothing there but a faint, cold boredom.

His mother had said something about his being responsible for Lisbet's new happiness. And Lee herself had seen Lisbet looking at him with loving radiance in her face. None of it made sense—unless he had generously given Lisbet up when her husband returned. Her mind simply reeled, trying to sort out conflicting clues.

On the way back to the office in Adam's car, she ventured to try and discuss it.

'I don't know Lisbet Carson well,' she said. 'But I'm glad her marriage seems to be going to work out after all.'

Rather bleakly, he said, 'Yes, some people are lucky enough to get a second chance.'

'Do you—know them well?' she ventured to ask.

'Scott is one of my best friends,' he answered.

Surprised, Lee said, 'I see,' thinking that she did. 'I didn't know.'

'You don't know much about me at all,' he said, snubbingly. 'You declined the offer, remember?'

As they neared the office car park, she said softly, 'Perhaps I've changed my mind.'

Adam drove into the park and stopped the car with a jerk, turning to face her. 'What?'

Lee didn't have the courage to repeat what she had said, only stared back into his angry eyes with what she hoped was some semblance of calm.

After a moment he said with soft contempt, 'More games, Lee?'

Numbly hurt, she shook her head, but he ignored her

mute denial. 'Did you have a fight with the boy-friend?'
he jeered. 'Or are you playing the field these days? The
offer is tempting,' he added, his eyes raking her with a
glance that made her shiver inwardly, 'but a little late.
There are some things that I don't believe in—sharing.'

He was looking at her as though he both hated her and
despised her, and she found she couldn't bear it. Unable
to answer him for the choking tears in her throat, she
opened the door and scrambled out: He made no attempt
to stop her as she fled across the car park and into the
building.

Later, when she had got over inwardly quivering with
hurt, she was able to feel resentful of that last remark. He
said he didn't believe in sharing, but he had seemingly expected her and Lisbet to share *his* favours, until her husband had arrived back on the scene. Did it make a difference
that he believed she hadn't known of his involvement with
Lisbet?

Again she was back to the problem of Lisbet. There were
things that made no sense—she felt as though she had
been trying to solve a puzzle with the wrong pieces. Or was
it that she was putting them together in the wrong order?
Could Lisbet possibly be happy with her husband when
only weeks ago she had obviously been in love with Adam?
And had Adam really cared for Lisbet—or was he relieved
that her husband had reclaimed her? Maybe he had *arranged* their reunion. Perhaps he had not intended marriage
at all, and had simply sidestepped it neatly when Lisbet
got serious, by bringing Scott back into her life and encouraging him to woo his wife again. If he had set out to
have an affair with her, he had been callous and unkind—
but then he had said once, 'I'm not kind. I thought you
knew.'

Whatever she knew about him, it had never been enough to understand him.

Some time during the afternoon it occurred to Lee that Brian Small might help her to sort out the confusion about Lisbet and Adam. It was he who had first suggested to her that they were seeing a lot of each other, and he who had been with her when she saw them together at the theatre. Besides, he always had his 'ear to the ground', as she was sure he would have said himself, and if she didn't have the right pieces of the puzzle, hardly anyone was more likely to be able to supply them.

She didn't see him that day, but in the morning she arrived early and loitered in the lobby, ashamed of herself for her curiosity, but determined, all the same, to satisfy it.

She saw Brian come in and managed to reach the lift just as he entered it, giving him a friendly smile.

'I haven't seen you for ages, Brian,' she said. 'How are things on *Holiday News*?'

'Booming,' he answered. 'But not as much as your part of the empire, I believe. Congratulations.'

'Thank you.' The lift was nearing her floor and she had no idea how to bring the conversation around to what she wanted so badly to discuss. Struck by a sudden idea, she said, 'I've been thinking of incorporating a travel page in *Lady*—could I pick your brains some time?'

Looking slightly surprised, Brian said, 'Sure. But wouldn't my editor be a better bet?'

Hastily she said, 'It's only half an idea at this stage. I don't want to do anything official yet. Would you mind?'

Brian shrugged, and she said, 'If you're free after work, shall we have a drink together? I won't keep you too long.'

He shrugged again and agreed, and Lee went to her office torn between relief and shame.

When they met that evening, she asked for his views on a travel page, and listened with half an ear while he gave them to her. When they were on their second drink and she felt he had exhausted his ideas she said casually, 'Oh, by the way, do you remember the night we saw Lisbet Carson? You said something about her being ready to marry again. We picked the wrong man, though—had you heard?'

'The wrong man?'

'I saw her yesterday,' Lee explained. 'With her husband. It seems that the marriage is on again.'

Brian looked thoroughly puzzled. 'That was obvious, wasn't it?' he asked. 'The night we saw them. I remember discussing it with you.'

Lee blinked. 'But—it was Adam she was with—wasn't it?' she faltered, remembering the other man, whose face she had not seen, who had walked over to the group beside Adam, and sat on the other side of Lisbet.

'Broome was there, yes. But it was her husband she was throwing loving glances at. You don't mean you didn't see him?'

'I only saw his back,' she said. 'I didn't realise——'

'I did think at one time that she might marry Adam Broome,' Brian added, 'but I should think he faded out of the running when her husband came back into the picture. I wonder if his nose is out of joint—though he seemed to be taking it pretty well, that night, wouldn't you say?'

'Oh, yes,' Lee agreed, scarcely knowing what she was saying. 'Yes, he certainly did.' It had all been very friendly.

Still uncertain and confused, she was beginning to wonder if anything was as it seemed. She had a ghastly feeling that somewhere or somehow she had been guilty of misjudging Adam, and that she might have done some irreparable damage to herself and him because of it.

It wasn't possible to go and ask him to explain, even if he had not treated her lately with obvious dislike and disdain. She began in the midst of her misery seriously to consider if she should resign and start looking for another job.

CHAPTER THIRTEEN

MICHAEL had indeed been offered a place in the student house that Janet and several friends shared. He seemed keen on the idea, and with some misgivings Lee gave it her blessing. One of the present tenants was moving out at the end of the term, and Michael would be taking his place.

The weather had become quite cool and wintry lately and Lee had begun to wear a coat to work. She was hurrying into the building one morning, head down and her collar held around her face against rain-laden wind, when she almost collided with Adam as they converged on the steps.

He held her arm to steady her, and didn't release it as they went towards the lift.

'I didn't see you in the car park,' he said, closing the door but not pressing the floor button.

'I came by bus,' she explained.

'You're very conscientious about conserving fuel, aren't you?' he asked. 'Or has your car broken down?'

'I sold it.'

As he looked askance, she said, 'I hardly ever used it, anyway, so there wasn't much point in keeping it.' She would have liked to tell him about Michael, but didn't know where to start.

She saw him looking at her coat, which was three years old and showing it, and he asked abruptly, with a small frown, 'Are you short of money?'

Swiftly she denied it, saying, 'No, of course not. You know I get a very good salary.'

'I know. I wondered what you——' But he didn't complete the sentence, and pushed the floor button rather viciously to take them up, turning away from her almost irritably.

To her surprise he got out on her floor, instead of continuing up.

She was early and Marion and Helen had not yet arrived, although one or two other early arrivals were sorting papers or perched on desks chatting as they passed through the outer office.

'Did you want to talk to me?' Lee asked, as Adam followed her into her own office.

'Yes, but there's no hurry,' he said. 'Take off your coat and get comfortable first.'

She opened the cupboard and stowed away her bag and began to unbutton her coat. Adam strolled over to the window behind her desk and stared out at the view. 'Some scientist quoted in this morning's paper reckons Rangitoto could erupt again,' he commented. 'It's only dormant, not extinct.'

'If it does, I'll have a good view, then, won't I?' she asked.

'You might have more than that,' he said, glancing round with a smile. 'Volcanoes can be dangerous.'

'I know.' Her hands stopped in their task as she gazed past him at the distant peak outlined against a hazy grey sky. 'It's hard to believe, though, that under that lovely graceful island there could be an enormous, hidden fire, trying to force its way out through the mountain. If it ever did escape, the entire island could disappear, I suppose.'

'Or at least blow its top. It's fascinating to think of, isn't it?'

'A bit scarey, though,' she said, slipping off her coat. 'All that sleeping fire ...'

Her sleeve caught on the strap of her watch, and she was trying to free it when the telephone rang on her desk.

'Oh—would you mind?' she said to Adam, looking up from the small problem.

Adam nodded and lifted the receiver. 'Miss Palmer's office,' he said crisply. Then, 'Yes. Just hold on a moment, will you.'

She had freed the coat and hung it up, and took the receiver from his outstretched hand.

Michael's hesitant, slurred voice said, 'Lee? I've lost a rather vital collection of notes. Have you seen a green folder about anywhere?'

'Would that be the one I saw on top of the refrigerator this morning?' she asked.

'What on earth is it doing there? Just a minute, I'll look,' he said, and she waited with a small, amused smile on her face until he returned to the phone. 'Got it! You're a wonder—I thought I'd looked everywhere.'

'You're lucky I happened to notice it while I was cooking your breakfast, lazybones,' she teased. Michael had been late rising that morning. 'You're going to be late, aren't you?'

'I'll just have time to get there if I leave the dishes. I know I said I'd do them, but——'

'All right, never mind,' she said. 'I'll do them when I get home, if you haven't got there before me.' She would do it much more quickly anyway, than he could virtually one-handed. She had only accepted his offer in the first place because she knew how he hated to feel useless.

'You're an angel, Lee,' he said fervently, and she laughed, saying,

'Yes, I know. 'Bye, love.'

'I take it that was *darling Michael*,' Adam's voice said harshly, recalling his presence in her office.

'Yes,' she said, thinking it was time this absurd mis-understanding was cleared up, but tonguetied by his hostile tone.

'How long has he been with you?' he asked, as though the words were dragged from him against his will. Surprised, she looked up at him, and he immediately said, 'Oh, never mind. It's none of my business, as you reminded me before.'

'Actually, a couple of months,' she said. 'But he'll be moving out soon.'

After a short, charged silence, Adam asked, 'Your idea —or his?'

'His, actually.' Moved by a spirit of mischief, Lee lowered her eyes to her desk, and added, 'He met another girl——'

The silence stretched longer this time, then he said very softly, 'Do you mind?'

'I'll miss him,' she said truthfully. 'But if that's what he wants——'

'You're very generous.'

'Not really.'

She didn't realise that he had moved until she felt his hand on her hair, then on her cheek, lifting her face, making her look at him.

'I'm sorry, Lee,' he said quietly, and she was shaken by the compassion in his eyes, and in his voice, 'but it may be for the best. Is he often like that at this hour of the morning?'

Blankly, she said, 'Like what?'

'Drunk,' he replied bluntly. 'Is it *your* money he spends on drink?'

Shamed by his sympathy and tenderness, she said calmly, 'He wasn't drunk. He talks like that because he has a partial paralysis caused by a birth injury. And,' she added, even as a ripple of shock passed over his face and his hand fell away, 'he's my brother.'

'Your brother,' Adam repeated slowly. He straightened and tipped back his head, putting a hand to the back of his neck. 'Oh, *lord*!' Then he dropped his hand and looked at her with gathering anger. 'Why the *hell* didn't you tell me? Instead of letting me think——'

Bewildered by his reactions, Lee said sharply, 'You gave me no chance to tell you—at least, not at first—and after that——' she shrugged. 'Well, it isn't really that important, is it?'

'Maybe not,' he said, coldly, after a moment. 'I'm aware that you don't hold much of an opinion of me. So I suppose it hardly matters what I think of you, does it?'

'I didn't mean that——'

'Oh, forget it!' he interrupted irritably. 'There's no need for excuses. You've already made yourself abundantly clear.'

Maybe she had, but *he* certainly hadn't, she was thinking as he abruptly changed the subject and began discussing business matters. With an effort she wrenched her mind back to everyday problems of magazine production.

It seemed to her that from then on Adam treated her with a cool indifference that was hardly less painful than the barely concealed contempt he had shown before. Life seemed suddenly flat, even professionally, since the excitement of the first issue of the new *Lady* faded, and sales steadily climbed.

She tried to forget the times that Adam had kissed her, his early suggestions of a deeper relationship between them. Maybe he had not, after all, been seriously interested in Lisbet, and perhaps if Lee had been less careful of her pride and more willing to turn a blind eye he might have come to love her as well as desire her. All the might-have-beens——

Finally she came to the conclusion that she must take some action, and she went to his office one morning holding a slim white envelope which she placed on his desk, saying, 'I've come to hand you my resignation.'

Adam glanced down at the envelope and then looked up at her without touching it.

'Why?' he asked abruptly.

'I—feel it's time I moved on.'

'That's no answer. Aren't you happy here?'

'That has nothing to do with it. I suppose since the magazine in its new form has taken off, I no longer feel challenged. I want to try something new.'

'Do you have another job in view?'

'Not yet. But I'll find something.'

He picked up the envelope, and a sudden smile crossed his face, as though he had just thought of something that pleased him. 'I've no doubt that you will. You're a girl of many talents.'

She wasn't sure if he was implying a double meaning there. She watched him tapping the envelope against his thumb, and in spite of herself almost winced when he said, 'Very well, Miss Palmer, I accept your resignation. When do you want to leave?'

'I'll give you time to find a replacement,' she said, keeping her voice steady with an effort.

'I'll get one as soon as I possibly can.'

Hurt, she tried to sound flippant. 'You sound almost glad to get rid of me,' she observed.

'Almost,' he replied, with laughter in his face, and she hated him momentarily for not hiding it.

Stiffly, she said she hoped he would find someone soon, and then left him before she betrayed how he had hurt her.

She hardly saw Adam before she left the firm, with as little fuss as possible. She couldn't stop the staff taking up a collection and presenting her with a magnificent gold pen and pencil set, but they heeded her sincere and fervently expressed preference *not* to have any formal farewell ceremonies, and although she steeled herself for a visit from Adam to shake her hand and wish her well, he didn't come. His secretary called just before five to say that he had left a message in case he didn't get back from a meeting he had attended that afternoon, and Lee scarcely took in the politely worded apology and good wishes. She supposed he would eventually send a note, dictated to his secretary, in appreciation of her service to the firm.

She might easily never see him again, and the thought made her panic. With some effort she brought herself under control.

By the time she got home she was calm and able to greet Michael with reasonable cheerfulness.

'No more grindstone for you?' he asked. 'What's it like being a lady of leisure?'

'I haven't had time to find out yet,' she pointed out mildly. 'Anyway, I hope it won't be for long. I have an appointment next Monday for an interview.'

'Got any plans for tonight?' he asked. 'Janet and the gang are going to a film. We're invited if you feel like it.'

Touched, she said, 'You go. I think I'll have an early night. Tying up loose ends all day has been a bit exhausting.'

'Oh, I'm not all that keen,' he said quickly, with brave dishonesty.

'I don't need company and comfort, love,' she said. 'Honestly. You go and enjoy yourself.'

'Are you sure? You look a bit—down.'

'Anti-climax,' she explained. 'Truly, no offence meant, I think I'd rather be alone.'

'Okay.' He began to go towards the bathroom, then turned. 'We haven't seen so much of Mark lately, have we?'

'Well, since you have a car now——'

'He was more interested in you than me. Did you have a row or something?'

'No, nothing like that.'

He limped towards her. 'I don't want to be nosey, but I know you haven't been too happy lately. If it's Mark, I could invite him round——'

'It *isn't* Mark! It's sweet of you to think of it, but please don't invite him for my sake. My life is complicated enough——'

Puzzled, he said, 'Okay, then. But if I can do anything——'

'I know. Thanks, Michael.'

When they had eaten and he had gone out to meet his friends, Lee did the dishes and then switched on the television, but the programmes seemed uninteresting and eventually she switched it off and decided to have a long hot shower and wash her hair.

She had switched on the set again while she used the small hand-drier, and was combing her newly-washed hair into silky curves when the doorbell rang. Tempted to pretend there was no one home, she stilled, wondering who on earth could be calling on them at this hour. Not that it was so very late, she realised, glancing at the clock. The evening had gone slowly.

The bell pealed again, and reluctantly she tightened the belt of the robe she was wearing over nothing but brief panties, and opened the door a crack.

'Are you going to let me in?' Adam asked, putting his hand on the door to push it wider.

Lee stepped back and he walked in, closing the door behind him.

'That outfit is beginning to look quite familiar,' he commented, his eyes glinting as they passed over her.

'I wasn't expecting visitors,' she said. 'I was planning an early night.'

'Do you want me to go?'

'Of course not,' she said, but couldn't imagine why he had come. 'Come and—sit down.' She waited until he had done so, on one of the comfortable armchairs, then said, 'Can I give you something to drink while I—put on some clothes?'

'No, thanks. Why bother, anyway? I've seen you in that before, as I just reminded you. It covers a good deal more than that bikini you wore when we went swimming.'

'There's nothing wrong with my bikini,' she said defensively. It was in fact quite modest as bikinis went.

'Did I say there was?' he asked. 'As a matter of fact, I concur with your opinion—wholeheartedly.'

Lee wished he wouldn't tease. It confused her, making her long to respond in kind, but not knowing where that might lead.

'I'm sorry I wasn't there this afternoon,' he said, as she sat down on the edge of the sofa. 'I meant to bring you home, actually.'

'There's no need to apologise,' she shrugged. 'Your

secretary gave your message to me. I quite understood.'

'I have something for you,' he said, standing up and taking a long narrow package from his pocket.

He crossed to sit beside her and began to open the package himself, handing her the red leather box inside.

She said, 'I've already been given a bonus.'

'I wanted to give you something a little more personal as well. Now that you no longer work for me,' he added deliberately. 'Open it.'

The opened lid revealed a gold watch, dainty and elegant, with tiny diamond chips around the face, and obviously very expensive. As she sat silent, he said, 'Call it a golden handshake.'

Lee looked up quickly, remembering how she had taunted him when Pat Blyth left, but he was smiling faintly without rancour.

'Put it on,' he said, taking it out of the box, and taking her wrist in his hand.

She pulled away. 'I can't——'

Firmly he grasped her wrist again, placing the watch under his hand and fastening it with the other before he let her go. 'Don't you like it?'

'Of course. It's beautiful, but far too expensive.'

'You've done a good job,' he said. 'The firm owes it to you.'

'Is this from the firm?' she asked in a low voice.

'I chose it. The firm pays. Does that satisfy your Victorian sense of propriety?'

When he put it like that she could hardly refuse. 'Thank you,' she said. 'Thank you very much.'

He picked up her wrist again and ran his thumb over the diamonds. 'It suits you. I knew it would.'

Diamonds. 'It isn't what I'm used to,' she said, faintly

smiling. Adam's hand was still holding her wrist, warm and firm, and she didn't want him to take it away. She sat very still, watching the tiny second hand of the watch go round and round, ticking away his time with her.

The telephone bell shrilled into the silence so suddenly that she jumped. Adam's hand fell away, and she got up quickly and lifted the receiver.

'Hi, Lee,' said Mark's voice. 'I ran into young Michael. He said you've left your job. Right?'

'Hallo, Mark. Yes, I have.'

'I have a friend who has a friend in the newspaper business. Apparently there's a job coming up for a lady editor—women's page or something. Would you like me to mention your name?'

'I *am* looking for a job,' she said. 'Could you find out more?'

'Sure thing. I'll let you know. Hey, I've missed you lately. When can I see you again?'

'You know we're always glad to see you,' she said.

'Not quite what I meant,' he said. 'Mike said he left you at home on your own. Are you lonesome?'

'No,' she said, smiling a little. Mark was likeable and she didn't want to see Michael hurt by losing his friendship. 'I'm not lonesome.'

'Sure you wouldn't like me to come round and keep you company?'

'No, thanks, not tonight.'

'Okay,' he said quite cheerfully. 'See you around.'

'Yes,' she said. 'Goodnight, Mark.'

Adam had stood up, and was watching her as she returned to the sofa. She sat down, but he remained on his feet, looking faintly brooding.

'So it's Mark,' he said. 'Not Mike.'

'What?'

'I heard you talking to Mark once before. Later I thought I'd mistaken the sound of "Mike" for "Mark". You sounded very affectionate, I remember.'

'Did I?' Lee was bemused, and couldn't remember on what occasion she had been speaking to Mark in front of Adam. 'He's an old friend. We used to be at school together.'

'Oh, yes, the old flame from the past. I remember you singing his praises to Helen on one occasion. You called him darling,' he added, making it sound like an accusation.

'I'm sure I didn't!' she protested.

'It was "hello, Mark", "Goodbye, darling",' he insisted.

'The only man I've ever called darling is my brother.'

'Then perhaps it was "Mike",' he said slowly.

'No. I've never called him Mike.' She looked up at him questioningly. 'When was this, anyway?'

'The night we did the television show. Don't you remember?'

'I've tried to forget that night,' she said, and a shadow crossed his face. Hastily she added, 'It was both of them. Michael watched the show at Mark's flat. Mark spoke to me first, then put Michael on the line.'

'I see. Not that it makes much difference, I suppose.'

Not sure what he meant by that, Lee agreed, 'I suppose not.'

Sensing tension in him, she said, 'Are you sure you wouldn't like a drink?'

'I'll get it—with your permission,' he said, swinging away from her to the little kauri table. 'Can I get you something?'

'I'll have a sherry,' she said.

Adam came back with two glasses in his hands and

handed her one as he sat down again. He drank his quickly and in silence while she toyed with hers. The tension in the air did not ease.

Lee kept her eyes down on her glass, but she could see the outline of his thighs straining against the material of his trousers, and his hand resting on one, the fingers strong and tanned. He leaned forward and put his glass on a nearby occasional table, and then shifted so that his hand was near her hair, his arm thrown along the back of the sofa.

'Drink up,' he said softly.

Obediently she sipped at her sherry, and he watched until she had finished it, apparently in no hurry. Then he took the glass and put it beside his own.

'Your hair looks very soft,' he said. He still sat in the same position, not touching her at all, so why should she have the distinct feeling that he was making love to her?

'I've just washed it,' she said, mesmerised by his eyes, that weren't cold at all, but darkened and strangely tender.

'Do you still dislike me, Lee?' he asked.

She opened her mouth in protest, but was unable to make a sound. The way he was looking at her was too disturbing. In the end she just shook her head.

'That wasn't very convincing,' Adam said wryly, and his hand slipped to her hair, stroking its fine softness, lifting it and letting it fall again, his eyes inviting her to convince him.

Tempted to throw herself into his arms, she determinedly looked away from his eyes, glancing down at her own hands, that she saw were locked together in her lap. Deliberately she loosened them, and shook her head to free it from his teasing fingers in her hair.

It didn't work. Adam's fingers tightened and he held

her, not cruelly but with determination, and made her turn her head to face him. But even the gentlest coercion was enough to make Lee resentful, and she set her teeth and wouldn't look at him.

He moved closer and releasing her hair, cupped her face in his hands. She looked at him defiantly as he stared into her eyes.

'Is Mark your boy-friend?' he asked quite softly.

'I go out with him sometimes.' She raised her hands and pulled his away.

'You used to go out with that guy from *Travel News*, too.'

'I've been out with quite a few men——'

'He said you threw him over for an old flame.'

'He was talking nonsense.'

'He was jealous.'

'Maybe he was, a little.'

'So was I.'

'*You!*'

'Envious, anyway. How important is Mark to you?'

Not very—not at all, compared to you. A desperate hope made Lee want to say it, but there were still unanswered questions, unsolved puzzles between them. And she was not at all sure what it was Adam really wanted of her. She made to get up, but he reached out and held her, her wrists imprisoned in one of his hands while his other arm pulled her against him and his body pressed her against the cushions of the sofa.

'Let me go!' she muttered, trying to twist out of his hold.

'I won't hurt you. Are you in love with Mark? Or anyone?'

How could she answer that? If she denied loving Mark, would he guess that she loved himself? And where would that leave them? Adam triumphant at her surrender, and she humiliated at having confessed love for a man who was merely salving his ego?

His hard-muscled warmth against her softness was confusing her mind, and she begged desperately, 'Adam, *please* let me go.'

'When you answer me,' he said, settling himself more comfortably against her.

Taking refuge in anger, she snapped, 'I won't answer until you let me go.'

Softly he laughed. 'I think I have the better bargain, my love,' he told her. 'I'm perfectly content to hold you like this until doomsday.'

His hand shifted from behind her back, and strayed inside the collar of her robe, slipping over her shoulder and back to her throat, his finger lingering in the hollow there, then sliding the robe from her shoulder exposing it to his wandering lips, exposing, too, the soft curve of her breast.

Clenching her teeth against her own urge to respond, she exclaimed, '*Don't!* Adam, *stop it!*'

His mouth was warm against her breast, and he suddenly let go her hands, sliding his around her waist. Lee put her hands on his hair, feeling its soft springing life under her fingers, and for a mad moment was tempted to press his head closer, to arch her body against his hands and let his lips move lower and take possession as she knew he wanted——

Instead, she closed her fingers and pulled at his hair, and he raised his head and rolled off her, turning away as he stood, and even from where she lay half-stunned, she could see the movement of his shoulders as he breathed deeply to regain his control.

As she sat up, pulling her robe about her almost viciously, he said in a thickened voice, 'I didn't mean to do that. I seem to make a habit of forcing myself on you. It isn't— my usual style.'

He turned to face her and she thought how handsome he looked, a slight flush under his tan, and his hair a little dishevelled. There would not be many women who would want to resist him.

Hardly knowing what she was saying, she asked, 'What *is* your usual style?'

He frowned, then smiled faintly. 'You don't really want to know.'

'I might,' she said softly. 'If I thought you were——' *serious,* was what she meant, but couldn't bring herself to say it, while he watched her with an intent look that unnerved her.

She stood up, and said, 'I think you'd better go.'

'If that's what you want,' he said, not moving at all.

Lee didn't mean to, but she heard herself saying, 'I'm not in love with Mark.'

Adam didn't show any change of expression, but his chest moved as though he had taken a deep breath, or sighed.

It suddenly occurred to her that she had questions of her own to ask, and after all, why shouldn't he answer them? 'Are you in love with Lisbet Carson?'

'In love with Lisbet?' he repeated blankly. 'Of course not!'

'Why *of course*?' she asked. 'She's lovely—and you saw a lot of her.'

'I saw a lot of her because she happens to be married to one of my best friends, who'd asked me to help him get her back.' Faint, cold anger showed in his eyes. 'I wouldn't have dreamed of making a play for Scott's wife!'

'That needn't stop you loving her.'

After a moment he said, 'I suppose not. The fact is, I don't. Not the way you mean.' He frowned. 'What on earth put that idea into your head, anyway?'

'When you asked me out to lunch,' she explained, 'I saw you meeting Lisbet, after you cancelled our date. You kissed her.'

'Very likely,' he agreed. 'On the cheek. I quite often do.'

'You——' Lee swallowed nervously, and then went on, 'You lied to me.'

'*No.*' She had made him angry. 'I tried to explain to you why I broke our date, but you wouldn't listen.'

'Because you lied,' she said steadily. 'I saw you and Lisbet. She was laughing. You told me you'd gone to meet a friend who was in trouble.'

Their eyes clashed, and Adam said, 'Get it right, Lee. I told you—started to tell you, I *had* a friend in trouble. The trouble was their broken marriage. Lisbet was in a state when she rang me that morning and asked me to meet her. Scott had sent a letter saying he was coming over, and she didn't feel ready to meet him. When I saw her she looked panic-stricken. I think I made some feeble joke to cheer her up and try to restore her sense of proportion. And yes, she did laugh.'

'I see.' Lee almost whispered it, ashamed of herself, and then she remembered something else.

'What is it?' he asked harshly, watching her expression.

Lee shook her head. 'Nothing.'

'Tell me. You might as well get it over with.'

'It's just—when Lisbet stayed at the beach—was she alone?'

'No.' Adam's mouth clamped on the word, then he added, 'Scott was with her. *I* went to a business convention that week. Is that what you wanted to know?'

'I'm sorry,' she whispered.

'Are you?' he said bleakly. 'Tell me something. If you thought I was in love with Lisbet, why did you think I was making love to *you*?'

'You said—something—once,' she said, 'about pique. I suppose I thought you were determined to prove that I wasn't completely indifferent to you after all.'

'And you're not?' he asked, very softly.

She couldn't read the expression in his eyes; they were narrowed and seemed to glitter. She couldn't speak, but he was waiting for her answer, and this was no time for prevarication. Very faintly, she shook her head.

At once he seemed to come to life. His eyes blazed as he came to her and took her shoulders in his hands, his fingers almost painful through the cloth. 'I don't know whether I should kill you or kiss you,' he gritted. 'I love you, you infuriating, provocative little witch. And you have the nerve to think that I've been stringing you along to gain some point for my pride! I've always known you didn't think much of me, but no matter your opinion of my character, at least you've admitted feeling *something* for me, even if it is against your better judgement. And I warn you, I'm going to fan that spark until it blazes into something that will set you aflame. One day you'll love me as I love you, and together we'll kindle a fire that never dies, that will warm us and our children for the rest of our lives.'

'Children?' echoed Lee, dazed.

'*Our* children. You're not one of those women who don't want any, are you?'

'No. Would it make a difference?'

'Not much.' He suddenly released her shoulders and pulled her close, and his voice became softer and almost pleading. 'I love you to distraction. You can have anything you want. I'm not going to ask you yet to marry me—I've got the cart before the horse now, haven't I?' He kissed her ear, and tipped back her head with his hand behind it. 'I want to court you, Lee—to woo you, until you learn to love me—please let me try. At least say yes to that.'

His sudden humility moved her as nothing else had, and she put up her hands and laughed a little as she pulled his head down, saying against his mouth, 'Yes, yes, yes to everything!'

She kissed him and rejoiced in his surprised response. He drew her closer, pressing her head against his hand with the passionate pressure of lips, then half lifted her until they were both ensconsed on the sofa, and when their mouths reluctantly parted, Lee was half lying across him, one hand supporting her, the other deliciously stroking the curves and hollows of her body.

'What do you mean, yes to everything?' he asked huskily, his lips softly tracing the outline of her mouth.

'Yes to letting you court me,' she said, whispering against his exploring lips. 'Yes to marriage—although you haven't asked me yet. Yes to loving you. Didn't you realise I already do?'

Adam lifted his head, looking into her eyes as though he couldn't quite believe her words. 'Convince me,' he said, and she smiled and said, 'When are you going to ask me to marry you? Must I wait very long?'

'Will you marry me?' he asked, almost demanded.

'Oh, yes, darling, I will!'

'You only call your brother that,' he said.

'And my husband,' she said. 'To-be,' she added, just before his lips touched her again and set her body aflame.

'He'll be home soon—my brother,' she explained when

his mouth left hers to wander across her cheek and find the hollow beneath her ear.

'Damn him,' Adam muttered. 'I want to marry you *soon*.'

'As soon as you like,' she promised. 'When did you decide that? To marry me, I mean.'

'The night I took you to Pauanui, when I kissed you and you responded so beautifully. Before that I knew I was crazily in love with you, but you were so determined not to let me near you—was it really so important not to get involved with the boss?'

'No,' she confessed. 'That was an excuse—because I thought you were—well, I'd seen you with Lisbet, and I thought you were only playing with me.'

'*Playing?* I was never more serious in my life. What sort of man do you think I am?' he demanded, leaning back to look at her face.

'The sort who can't resist kissing a girl he "finds in his arms"!' she explained. 'You told me so the very first day we met.'

'Oh, lord!' he groaned. 'As a matter of fact that was highly untypical, but I was powerfully attracted to you from the start. I was never more shattered than when you told me my attraction for you had faded—and never more glad to receive a resignation than I was to get yours.'

'I noticed,' Lee said drily. 'Did you have to make it so obvious?'

'Can you blame me for being pleased? It effectively removed the only excuse you had given me for your coolness towards me—apart from lack of—desire. And *that* didn't quite hold water after that little episode at the beach.' His eyes glittered with some small triumph into hers, bringing warmth to her cheeks. 'Why did you have to pretend it meant nothing to you?' His arms tightened on her as though promising punishment, and she said swiftly, 'I still thought you and Lisbet——'

Adam looked dangerously impatient, and she said, 'I misunderstood your mother, she said something about your being responsible for bringing Lisbet happiness again. And I'd already seen her apparently being affectionate to you at the theatre—I didn't realise her husband was there, too.'

'Lisbet is an affectionate girl, and demonstrative. If she was being affectionate it was only to show her gratitude for what she saw as my efforts to bring her and Scott together.' He looked down at her lying in his arms. '*You* were being rather affectionate yourself, with that twit from *Holiday News*.'

'Brian,' she said with dignity, 'is a very intelligent and clever journalist——'

'No doubt,' he interrupted. 'But I don't want to know. So shut up.'

He made sure she did, in the most pleasant way possible, hardly bothering to try and control his obvious desire, until she broke away and stood up shakily, pulling her robe together across her sensitive breasts while he watched, a lambent flame still flickering in his blue eyes.

'Michael——' she said, hearing the sound of his imminent approach outside.

'When we're married, he won't be around to rescue you,' said Adam, gently jibing.

'I won't want to be rescued,' she said, smiling mistily at him. 'I'd walk through fire with you.'

He stood up and tightly clasped her hand. 'The only fire we'll walk through will be of our own making,' he said. 'And I'll be with you every step of the way.'

And there's still *more* love in

Harlequin Presents...

Yes!

Six more spellbinding
romantic stories every month
by your favorite authors.
Elegant and sophisticated tales of
love and love's conflicts.

Let your imagination be swept away to
exotic places in search of adventure,
intrigue and romance. Get to
know the warm, true-to-life
characters. Share the special
kind of miracle that
love can be.

Don't miss out. Buy now and discover
the world of HARLEQUIN PRESENTS...